"Shhh!" Nicky whispered. "Somebody's coming up the hill."

Two lights swung in mid-air. Then, as they grew closer, I could make out two figures.

"Get as far back in the cave as you can!" Nicky whispered. "I never thought they'd find this cave!"

I could hear the fear in Nicky's voice. And knowing he was afraid made me afraid, too. I was more afraid than I'd ever been in my life.

Summer Cruise, Summer Love

by Alida E. Young

For Milly—
wonderful friend, teacher, and severest critic

Special thanks for all their help to the stu-
dents of Stone Creek Elementary School, Vista
Verde Middle School, and El Camino Real
School in Irvine, California. Also, many thanks
to the students of St. Catherine Laboure
School in Torrance, California.

Published by Willowisp Press, Inc.
401 E. Wilson Bridge Road, Worthington, Ohio 43085

Printed in the United States of America

10 9 8 7 6 5 4 3 2 1

ISBN 0-87406-451-1

One

I couldn't wait to tell my mom the news! My best friend Deanna had asked me— Kirstie Allen—to go to Greece with her family. My mom just *had* to let me go. She just had to!

"Mom! Mom!" I shouted as Deanna and I came running into the house. "Where are you?"

"I'm in the kitchen," she called.

As we burst into the kitchen, my mother asked with a sigh, "What have you done now, Kirstie?"

She always assumes I'm in some kind of trouble. "I haven't done anything," I said.

"That will be the day," my twin brother, Yancey, said.

I ignored him. His name is really Lance. But when I was little, I couldn't pronounce my *L*s, and I've called him Yancey ever since.

"Deanna's mom wants to know if I can go

5

to the Greek islands with their family. They're leaving in a few weeks, and I want to go more than anything in the world. Please, Mom, can I go?" I said all in one breath.

"Pleeease, Mrs. Allen," Deanna begged. "We're going to fly to Athens, and then take our new yacht to different islands. It won't cost Kirstie anything. Lance is invited, too— if he wants to go."

She tried to sound nonchalant, but I knew she wanted him to go. Deanna has a major crush on my dumb brother. I can't figure out why.

"Not me," Yancey said, and I saw Deanna's shoulders sag. "I'm going to basketball camp."

"We'll discuss it with your father and Deanna's parents," my mother said.

Well, at least she hadn't said no.

"Can Kirstie go to town with me now?" Deanna asked. "I'm going to buy a bathing suit and some shorts for the trip."

"All right. But Kirstie, be sure to be back by 4:00. We're going to the hospital to see your grandmother. She wants us to bring her some chop suey and more movie magazines."

"I'll be back in time," I said. "I promise." I wasn't going to do *anything* that might ruin my chances of going to Greece.

"And take an umbrella," Mom added. "It

looks like a storm's headed our way."

I picked up an umbrella without arguing. I was going to be the best daughter in southern California so that my parents would let me go to Greece.

We had to stop at Deanna's house to get her charge cards. My mother thinks it's awful that a 14 year old has her own credit cards.

The way my parents treat me, you'd think I was six years old. I'll be glad when I'm 18 and can do anything I want.

Deanna and I live next door to each other. I guess we've been friends practically forever. We like the same movies and music, the same books—everything. She's more like my twin than Yancey is.

Oh, sure, Deanna and I get angry with each other sometimes. It never lasts long, though. Deanna's always over being angry by the next day—even when she's right. You probably think it sounds goofy and mushy, but I'd just about die if we weren't friends anymore.

Our house is okay, but the Asburys' house is a regular mansion. They even have a riding stable, a tennis court, and a peated hool. I mean, a heated pool. That's another thing. I'm always getting my tang tungled. I mean my tongue tangled. Sometimes, it can be downright embarrassing. I used to do it on purpose to be funny. But now I do it without even thinking. My dad says that's how I do everything—without thinking.

When we stopped at Deanna's to get her credit cards, nobody was home except Mrs. Foley. She's the housekeeper, but she's more like one of the family. Ever since Deanna and I were little, Mrs. Foley has been the one who's bandaged our scrapes and cuts, the person we could talk to without getting yelled at.

Deanna's parents own a lot of buildings in San Diego. They're gone a lot. Her dad travels so often on business to foreign countries that Yancey thinks he's probably in the CIA. Yancey thinks everyone's in the CIA.

"This trip with your family is going to be the best vacation ever," I said.

"I just hope you don't get us into trouble like last year," Deanna said.

Last year, our families went to Yellowstone Park together. Deanna, Yancey, and I had gone on a hike, and I'd wanted to lead because I'd read the map carefully. I'd wanted to show everybody that I was responsible, but it didn't exactly work out that way.

Deanna giggled. "Remember how you got us lost? Lance tried to tell you that we were going in the wrong direction, but would you listen? No, not you. Once you've made up your mind, you might as well be deaf."

"I do listen. But how was I supposed to know that I'd looked at the map upside down? No matter what I do or how hard I try, something always goes wrong."

Deanna grinned. "That's okay, Kirstie. I like you just the way you are—klutzy."

"Deanna, I am *not* klutzy. Things just happen to me," I explained.

"It's just that when you get an idea, you charge ahead and never listen to anybody or think about what's going to happen."

Well, no matter what Deanna says, most of the time it's not my fault. Things just happen, like I said. "Come on," I said, looking up at the black clouds. "It looks like rain."

We were halfway into town when I realized I'd left the umbrella at Deanna's house.

I think Deanna and I tried on clothes in every shop in Rancho La Mira. We're both tall and have dark brown hair and eyes. We like the same things, except she goes for pale blues and pinks. I love bright colors, like yellow, red, and orange. It works out pretty well, because sometimes when I do feel like wearing pale colors, I can borrow Deanna's clothes. And she can borrow mine.

I picked out some things to show Mom. As I was trying on this great bracelet, I noticed

9

my watch said 3:25.

"Deanna! I lost track of time. I have to go right now, or I'll be late." I was trying to take off the jeans I'd been trying on, but they got stuck.

"If you'd take off your shoes first, you'd find it much easier," the saleswoman said with a nasty tone of voice as she walked by the dressing room.

"Uh, sorry," I told the woman, tugging on the jeans. I glanced at my watch again. "Deanna, can I charge these jeans on your card so I can just wear them home? I'll never get them off in time to be home by 4:00. I know Mom will let me buy them."

"Okay," Deanna said.

She charged our stuff, and since I couldn't get the jeans off over my shoes, the woman had to scan the sales ticket while the jeans were on me. I felt so dumb. The saleswoman took forever to ring up our stuff, but she finally finished. I grabbed some of Deanna's packages, and we ran out.

As we headed for Asbury Road (That's right, it's named after Deanna's family!), I had a really great idea.

"Let's take a shortcut through the airport," I said.

"You know we're not supposed to cut across

the airfield," Deanna said.

"I know," I said impatiently. The only problem with Deanna is that she's always afraid to do anything. "It won't hurt to do it this one time. It *is* a pretty small airport. And your dad's plane is stored in a hangar there, so we can say we just wanted to see it. Anyway, if I'm late, I might not get to go with you to Greece."

Deanna gave a big sigh, and I knew I'd won the argument. She hates it, but I can usually talk her into doing things.

We took off for the airport. At the fence that surrounded the airstrip, we stopped. I looked up at the sky, and I didn't see any planes coming in. There were plenty of big, dark rain clouds, though. And there weren't any planes on the runway ready to takeoff. I tossed the packages over the metal fence, and started to climb over.

"I still don't think we should do this," Deanna whispered. I don't know who she thought could hear us except some rabbits.

"Oh, stop arguing, Deanna. Let's go."

I was straddling the barbed wire at the top of the fence. It wasn't exactly a great position for holding a conversation. "Come on, Deanna! Nobody's going to see us if we hurry."

As I jumped down I heard the seat of my

jeans tear. "Oh, no!" My rear end had gotten caught on a barb. *Why did everything always go wrong*? All I'd wanted to do was to get home on time.

On top of everything, it started to rain really hard.

Deanna made it over the fence. "Look!" she cried when she hit the ground. "Somebody's running to a truck! They're coming after us!"

Deanna was right! Somebody was coming after us. "Hurry!" I yelled.

We grabbed our packages and were halfway across the runway when an airport security pickup truck zoomed up to us.

A guy in a uniform jumped out. "What in blue blazes do you kids think you're doing?" That's not exactly what he said. That's what my grandma would have said. The airport guy said something that I would have definitely gotten grounded for saying.

Deanna and I knew most of the airport people, but I'd never seen this guy before. "This is Deanna Asbury," I said, nodding toward her. "Her father practically built this airport, and I don't think he'd apprec—"

"I don't care if her dad's the president of the United States!" he yelled, interrupting me. "Get in!" He pointed to the truck. "I think her dad will want to know about this."

12

"Oh, no!" Deanna wailed. "Do you have to tell him?" Then she looked at me. "Kirstie Lee Allen, you're always getting us into trouble!"

"Please, sir, she's right," I said. "It's not her fault that we're out here. Just let us go, and we promise never to cross the runway again."

"Get in the truck," he said again. "If it's your fault, we'll call *your* dad instead."

I'd really blown it. I thought that maybe they'd fine us—or even send us to jail. At the very least, I was in big trouble with Mom and Dad. And Deanna would probably never speak to me again. Good-bye Greece!

The man asked for my phone number. I glanced at my watch. It was after 4:00. Mom and Dad would be waiting for me to go to the hospital. I thought about giving him a wrong number, but I figured that wouldn't help.

I couldn't hear much of what he said to my dad, except, "I think you'd better come down here, Mr. Allen."

I was so worried that I couldn't think of any good excuses before my whole family showed up. That was all I needed—to have Yancey making smart remarks about the trouble I was in again. Mrs. Foley came to take Deanna home. She didn't say anything. She just gave me a sad, disappointed look and shook her head.

Mom and Dad didn't say anything to me in front of the others, either. But Mom's lips were in a tight line, and the little muscles along Dad's jaw were jumping like crazy. Those things always mean they're angry. Believe me, I'm an expert at telling when Mom and Dad are angry.

Mom and Dad and Mrs. Foley went into an office and talked to the airport man for a few minutes, but I couldn't hear a word they said. When they finally came out, Dad took my arm—not very gently—and started to steer me out to our car. I looked back at Deanna, but she didn't look up. "I'm sorry," I called.

She didn't answer. I knew she was really mad at me this time. She probably didn't want me to go to Greece with her at all.

In the car I asked, "What are the airport people going to do to us?"

"*They* aren't going to do anything," Dad said with a frown.

Uh-oh. I slunked down in my seat, wondering what kind of punishment my parents had in mind for me. The closest I was going to get to Greece this summer was if I never washed my hair!

Two

ALL the way to the hospital I'd tried to tell Mom and Dad I was sorry and that I'd just wanted to get home on time. To hear them talk, you'd think I'd gotten into trouble on purpose.

"Grandma Lillian," I said and nodded toward Mom and Dad when we walked into the hospital room. "Please tell them to let me go to Greece. You've told me it's the most beautiful, romantic place in the world."

"You're really something, Kirstie," Yancey said. "You haven't even asked Grandma how she feels."

"I feel just fine," Grandma said, throwing her gossip magazine on the floor. "No broken hip's going to keep me down."

Grandma fell off a horse a couple of weeks ago. A couple years ago she broke her leg skiing. She tries to do everything. I mean, my grandmother has ridden a motorcycle, water skied, climbed mountains—you name it, and she's done it.

"Now, let me have that chop suey, and tell me more about this trip to Greece," she said.

"I'd be going with the Asburys on their new yacht," I answered. "They're leaving in a couple of weeks, and they'll be staying for a whole month."

"Why shouldn't she go?" Grandma demanded to know, looking at my parents.

I grinned. I knew she'd be on my side. She and Grandpa had spent their honeymoon in the Greek islands.

"We don't think Kirstie has shown that she's responsible enough to go on a month's trip," Mom told Grandma. "We've just come from the airport. Kirstie and Deanna were caught on the runway."

I'll bet if it had been Yancey who was caught on the runway, they'd still let him go to Greece. He's only 15 minutes older than I am, but he gets to do lots more things. Maybe it's because he's a boy. But it's sure not fair.

"If you let me go, I won't do anything without asking the Asburys first. I'll be responsible. I'll be absolutely perfect."

"Oh, right!" Yancey said.

"Are you going?" Grandma asked, pointing

at Yancey with her chopsticks.

"Nope. I'm going to basketball camp," he answered.

Grandma sat up more in bed. She pointed the chopsticks at Mom and Dad and gave them a stern look. "Did it ever occur to you two that if you'd give Kirstie more responsibility, she might act more responsibly?"

"Kirstie never thinks before she acts," Mom said. "And she never listens to anything anyone tries to tell her."

"I do, too," I said. "It's not my fault if sometimes my plans don't work out the way I think they will."

"Well, if you ask me..." Grandma held up her hand. "And I know you didn't ask me. But I think you should ground her for the next couple of weeks."

"Grandma!" I wailed.

"And then you should let her go to Greece. It's too good an experience to pass up."

I let out a whoop!

"And she'll probably get into trouble just the same way you always did on your trips," Dad told Grandma, shaking his head.

Grandma has been all over the world. When she got caught in a revolution in Iran, we thought we'd never see her again. Yancey used to say that she must be a spy to travel around the way she does. But then, he thinks everybody's a spy.

"Please, Dad, give me any kind of punishment you want. But let me go to Greece."

"We'll have to think a lot more about it," Dad said. But I thought there was a tiny smidgen of hope in his voice. Maybe, just maybe, they'd let me go. He kissed Grandma. "Ellen and I want to talk to the doctor, to see how much longer you have to be here."

When Mom and Dad left the room, I pushed aside all of Grandma's movie magazines and sat on the edge of the bed. She set aside the carton of chop suey and the chopsticks and took my hands. "If you'll get my photo album from home," she said, "I'll show you all the places to go when you're in Greece."

I nodded. Grandma had told me all about Greece, but I never got tired of hearing her talk about her travels. "You'll have a fantastic time in Greece, Kirstie. I wish I could stow away on the yacht and go with you."

She looked over at Yancey, who had turned on the TV. "I'd think you'd want to go, too, Lance. You'd have a great time."

I was glad that he wasn't going. I wanted him to stay home and go to his stupid basketball camp. But then I realized that if he decided to go, Deanna wouldn't be able to stay angry with me.

"Yeah, Lance, come on." I never call him Yancey to his face. He hates it. "It'll be a blast."

"Who wants to see all that romantic junk?" he asked.

"You love sports," Grandma said slyly. "If you go to Greece, you might get to see where they held the very first Olympic games."

"And you've always wanted to learn to sail," I added. "I'll bet Mr. Asbury would teach you how to handle the yacht."

"Yeah?" he asked, acting a little bit interested.

"You can snorkel and mess around in caves," Grandma told him.

"Well, maybe I'll think about it," he said.

As my parents came back into the room, I leaned over and whispered, "Thanks, Grandma Lillian. You're the greatest."

"Bring me a souvenir," she whispered back. "And if you do get into trouble, call me."

* * * * *

Well, Mom and Dad took Grandma Lillian's advice, like I thought they would. I was grounded for two weeks. That was really boring. But I survived it, partly by looking at

Grandma's photo albums of Greece. And Yancey decided to go, after all. I guess basketball camp could wait.

So, after what seemed like a long, long time, there we were—sitting on the plane, on our way to Greece. As I looked out the window of the 747, I felt as if we were a ship sailing on white clouds.

Mrs. Foley, Yancey, Deanna, and I were playing games. But I was too excited to concentrate on the game. I kept making mistakes, and Yancey kept yelling at me.

I got up to stretch my legs by walking in the aisles. I'm always hungry, so I took my glass of soda pop and bag of nuts with me.

A woman in the front row stood up to get something out of the overhead storage. I thought she looked familiar. She caught my eye and gave me a dazzling smile. She was beautiful—tall and slim and dressed like a model in a fashion magazine.

I hurried back to my seat and poked Deanna. "Can you see that woman in the front row?" I whispered. "Do you recognize her?"

Deanna shrugged. "She looks like a movie star, or one of those people on that show about the rich and famous. I think I saw a show about her couch once."

"I'll bet that's where I've seen her. I'm going

to get her autograph," I said, holding the bag of nuts in my teeth so I could dig my notebook out of my bag.

"You can't do that!" Deanna cried. "You don't even know her name."

I dropped the nuts on my seat so I could answer. "I'll know her name after I get her autograph," I said. "I just know she's somebody famous. Grandma Lillian goes crazy over autographs."

The plane bumped, and I nearly spilled my drink on Deanna.

"You'd better give me your glass while you go up front," Deanna said.

"Don't worry. I'll be careful."

I made my way up to the front row and smiled at the woman. She looked even more perfect close up. She was wearing a white silk suit that looked like it cost a lot. The man beside her looked really rich, like he was an English duke or something.

I held out my notebook to the woman. "I'm sorry to bother you, but I know I've seen you on TV or in a movie."

She turned that dazzling smile on me again. "I've only been in one movie. It was *Terror at Midnight*."

"I knew I'd seen you," I said. "You were wonder—" I stopped myself, just as I remembered that I'd seen the movie all right. And she'd been killed in the first scene. "You were a beautiful corpse. I mean, you died just great. Umm, I mean, would you mind signing your autograph for me?"

"I'd be happy to," she said.

As she signed her name with a gold pen, I wished I had pretty hands and long fingernails like hers. I smiled at the man. "Are you anybody. I mean—" My face must have turned fire-engine red. "I mean, are you an actor, too?"

He laughed. "I don't think you've heard of me. I'm Gerald Burke—Jerry to my friends. I manage Miss Loring's affairs."

I had expected him to have one of those fancy English names, like Sir Wilfred Hyde-Bottom.

As she handed the notebook back to me, I glanced at her name. It was Sonia Loring. Just then, the plane shuddered and dipped. You guessed it—my cola splashed all over her beautiful suit. "I'm so sorry," I said. "Oh, your suit! It's ruined!"

I wanted to hide under the seat, jump out the window without a parachute—anything to get out of that embarrassing situation! Why did things like this always happen to me? How was I supposed to know the plane would bounce like a rubber ball? All I'd wanted was to get an autograph for Grandma. "I'm sorry— honest."

"Don't worry about it," she said, not even sounding angry. "I brought plenty of clothes with me."

The plane quivered and bounced again. "I'd better go back to my seat before I land in your lap. Thanks for the autograph, and thanks for being so nice."

I hurried to my seat and waved the notebook at Deanna and Yancey. "She *is* a movie star. Grandma Lillian's going to go bonkers."

Deanna's mom turned around in her seat. "Kirstie, did you spill your drink on those people up front?"

"Uh, yes, but they weren't angry or anything."

Yancey shook his head like he couldn't believe what had happened. "Hey, no problem," he said in an actress voice. "Here's a spot you missed. Would you mind throwing a little more soda right here?"

"Knock it off, Lance," I ordered.

"Try to be more careful," Mr. Asbury said.

The pilot's voice came over the speaker. "Ladies and gentlemen, we're heading into some rough weather, but we may be able to climb above it. There's nothing to worry about, but please keep your seat belts fastened."

For the next hour the plane bounced and dipped. I hung onto the arm rest so tightly that my fingers hurt. Noticing that Deanna looked scared, I forced a smile.

"Hey, this is better than a roller coaster ride." I said as I reached over and squeezed her hand. "Remember how scared I was when we rode the Matterhorn at Disneyland?"

She giggled nervously. "Yes, but you made us ride it six times."

"And I was the one who got sick, too."

We got to laughing about some of our adventures together, and the plane trip went faster. But when we finally landed in Athens, I didn't want to ever see another plane again.

As we came out of the airport customs area we saw Miss Loring and her manager again. Even Yancey was pretty impressed by her. "Close your mouth," I whispered. "You look like a guppy."

A bearded, hulky-looking man in a Greek fisherman's hat and mirrored sunglasses came up to her. He looked like a weight lifter. He kept looking around as if he were afraid somebody was watching him. When he handed Miss Loring a piece of paper, I figured he was kind of embarrassed about asking for her autograph. I thought it must be fun to have people always wanting you to sign your name.

Just then, a man hurried up to us. "Mr. Asbury!" he said. "I have some bad news. We've had a terrible storm here. Many of the boats were smashed against the docks. The mast of the *Deanna* was split, and her hull is damaged."

"Oh, no!" Deanna cried.

I felt awful for her. She'd been so happy to have a boat named after her.

Mr. Asbury introduced the man as the skipper who had brought the yacht to Greece. "How long will it take to repair her?" Mr. Asbury asked.

"It will take a couple of weeks, at least. It might take even longer."

Deanna's mother sighed. "What do we do now?"

"I suppose we could get on one of those cruise ships," Deanna's dad said.

Mrs. Asbury shook her head. "I don't like that idea. I want the kids to see the real Greece. On one of those ships a thousand people get off at each island."

"I'll see if I can rent a yacht for a couple of weeks," Mr. Asbury said.

That sounded like a good idea. I started to feel better.

The skipper shook his head. "I already checked. Most of the yachts were damaged, and those that weren't damaged are already booked."

Mrs. Foley put her arms around Deanna and me. I knew she was disappointed, but she was trying to comfort us.

"I'm sorry, Kirstie," Deanna said to me. "I know how much this trip means to you."

I did feel bad. But I felt even worse about the yacht. "Don't worry," I whispered to her. "I'll bet they can fix the *Deanna* so that it's better than new."

Yancey tried to make a joke. "Well, at least Kirstie didn't have anything to do with it."

Deanna gave him a weak smile.

Miss Loring and her manager had been standing to the side. As they started over to us, Yancey made a joke in our secret twin language about Jerry Burke's cane.

Deanna looked puzzled, like she usually does when Yancey and I use our language. "What do you mean?" she asked.

Yancey and I laughed. Ever since we were little we've used our own language. It drives Mom and Dad crazy. Deanna's never been able to learn it. Sometimes when we don't want anybody else to know what we're talking about, we still use it. I whispered to Deanna,

"Yancey thinks Mr. Burke looks weird carrying that cane."

The dark spot on Sonia's skirt looked awful. "I'm really sorry," I said to her. "Your suit is ruined."

"Please send the bill to us," Mr. Asbury told her. "We're staying at the Ariadne Hotel."

Miss Loring smiled at me. "It wasn't her fault that the plane dipped at the wrong moment."

At last, somebody who understood.

"Please, just forget it," she said.

She wasn't only beautiful, but she was nice, too. Then I remembered my manners. "Miss Loring," I said, "This is Mr. and Mrs. Asbury, Mrs. Foley, my friend Deanna, and my brother Lance."

Then I nodded toward Mr. Burke to introduce him to everyone. "And this is Miss Loring's manager, Mr. Berry Jerk—"

I closed my eyes. I couldn't believe I'd said it. "I mean, Jerry Burke," I mumbled as they all laughed. The only jerk in the place was me. Miss Loring would think I was an idiot.

"We overheard you talking about your yacht," Miss Loring said. "If I may make a suggestion, Mr. Burke and I are taking a yacht on the Apollo Tours. There are only about 16 people, and they stay in small, non-touristy hotels. I think the kids would love it."

"Oh, Daddy, can we?" Deanna begged.

"We're booked on Apollo II, heading to Santorini and Mykonos," Mr. Burke said. "You might be able to take that tour."

"Oh, Mom, please?" Deanna asked again.

Before I knew it, it was all settled. Mr. Asbury would stay in Athens until the yacht was repaired, and then he'd pick us up at one of the islands. They thanked Miss Loring for telling us about the tour.

"I hope we'll see you again," Miss Loring said. "Have a wonderful vacation."

I sighed as I watched them leave. They made a perfect pair. Mr. Burke was tall and thin. He clicked the tip of his cane on the floor as he walked. Every head in the place turned to look at them. "If I could be like her, I'd never ask for another thing in my entire life," I said to Deanna and Yancey. "They're incredible," I said as we all watched the couple walk away.

"Humph!" Yancey snorted. "He's probably got a knife in the end of that cane."

I gave him a dirty look. "Oh, chill out, Yancey," I said. "You've been watching too many spy movies."

Three

BECAUSE of the storm damage to the yachts, all the tours were almost full. There were only four openings left on the Apollo II, so Deanna's mom did a really nice thing. She asked Mrs. Foley if she'd take us kids. Mrs. Foley had never been on a big trip like this before.

Because of the storm that had hit the islands, no planes were flying. We had to take a ferry to meet the Apollo II. So we took a bus to the port. Up ahead of us at the dock, we saw the gigantic ferry boat. Together with the rest of the tourists, we poured into the ferry like ants going into an anthill.

Mrs. Foley, Deanna, Yancey, and I sat down at a table in the lounge. The table seemed to be tilting from side to side.

"Is it okay if I go up on deck?" I asked Mrs. Foley.

"Sure, but be careful," she said. "The sea looks rough, and the wind's really blowing."

I looked at Deanna and Yancey. "Do you guys want to come?"

They both shook their heads. "I'm not feeling so hot," Deanna said.

I went up to the deserted top deck. Mrs. Foley was right about the rough sea and wind. I had to brace my legs and push against the wind to get to the rail. The waves were humongous. The cold, salty spray stung my face. I felt great. I held up my arms and shouted into the wind, "I'm really here! I'm really in Greece!"

"Don't you feel like you're on top of the world?" a voice asked from behind me.

I put my arms down and turned around, my face bright red with embarrassment. In front of me was Miss Loring.

"When I'm in Greece, I always feel as if the old Greek gods are watching over me," she said with that fantastic smile of hers. She was dressed in jeans and a windbreaker. But she looked just as great as she'd looked in her silk suit. Actually, she looked better, because the silk suit had my cola all over it!

"That's what my grandma says," I answered.

"I just knew the two of us would have a lot in common," Sonia said, looking at me.

Oh, right, I thought. *We sure do have a lot in common. You're rich and beautiful and talented and famous—just like me!*

"Are you going on one of the Apollo tours?" she asked.

I nodded. "We're going on the same one as you are."

"That's wonderful. I think fate has thrown us together."

I absolutely couldn't believe it! This movie star was talking to me like we were old buddies. And what would Grandma think when she found out I was traveling with a movie star. She'd flip out for sure!

"Are you on a vacation?" I asked.

"It's part vacation and part work. We're looking for a good place to shoot a movie."

"Wow," I said. "You're doing another movie? I'm sure it'll be as good as *Terror at Midnight.* Will you play another dead person?" What a stupid thing to say, but I couldn't help it.

"My grandma loves the movies. Wow, I sure wish she could meet you. She and Grandpa spent their honeymoon in Greece."

Miss Loring looked around to see if we were alone. She moved closer and said softly, "Jerry and I are on our honeymoon, too."

It was so romantic I just wanted to die. I couldn't wait to tell Deanna.

"No one knows, so promise me you'll keep it a secret," she whispered.

"Where do you live?" she asked.

"I live in Rancho La Mira in southern California. It's not too far from San Diego. Everybody grows avocados where I live."

I stopped. What an idiot I was. I mean, there I was, talking to a famous person, and I was blabbing about avocados!

But she smiled as if she didn't mind me being the biggest nerd in the solar system. After we looked at the sea for a while, she said, "You and Yancey look about the same age."

"We're fraternal twins. I'm a girl, and he's a boy, so we're not identical." Thanks for explaining that, Kirstie, I thought. She probably hadn't noticed! I just opened my mouth, and dumb stuff came pouring out. Maybe I was a little nervous talking to a movie star.

I told her all about my family. She really seemed interested. It wasn't like she was listening just to be polite. But then I realized that I was talking too much about myself.

"Umm, what about you, Miss Loring?" I asked. "Do you live in Hollywood or Beverly Hills?"

"Please call me Sonia," she said.

Please call me Sonia! Can you believe it?

It was all I could do to keep from fainting and falling overboard!

"I have a condo in Hollywood," Sonia said. "But I've been living in hotels recently...because I've been traveling so much."

"My grandma loves to travel. She's been everywhere," I said.

"Your grandmother sounds like quite a lady. You're lucky," Sonia said. "I don't have any family left, except Jerry, of course. I had a sister, but she died when she was just about your age. You remind me of Jeanie. That was my sister's name."

She paused and looked out at the waves for a minute. Then she said brightly, "I guess you've been a lot of places, too?"

I shook my head. "No, I haven't. And if it hadn't been for Deanna, I wouldn't be on this trip."

"At first I thought Deanna was your sister."

"Well, we practically are sisters," I answered, "only better. Sometimes I drive her crazy, but she never gets *really* angry with me."

Now that the ferry was out in the open sea, the wind was getting so bad that we could hardly stand up.

"I think we should go below," Sonia said. "We don't want to be swept overboard."

We slipped and struggled down the ladder. As we came into the lounge, the room felt hot and stuffy. "I'll see you later," Sonia said. Then she gave me that beautiful smile. "I have a feeling you and I are going to become good friends. I hope you have room in your heart for one more friend."

What a beautiful thing to say. I nodded, but I couldn't even say anything. This was all too unbelievable. A glamorous movie star was hoping I had room in my heart for her! *Don't worry, I'll make room!*

* * * * *

It was almost evening when we reached the port where we would transfer to the Apollo II. Yancey, Deanna, Mrs. Foley, and I walked to the boat through the harbor. I hurried on ahead and ran up the gangplank to the boat, nearly bumping into two people waiting at the top.

A handsome man in a uniform caught me. "Welcome aboard, Miss," he said. "Captain Tombazi, at your service."

"I'm sorry," I said. "I just couldn't wait."

I glanced at the guy beside him who was grinning at me. He had blond curly hair, deep blue eyes, dimples, and looked about 16 years old. He also was incredibly cute.

The captain nodded toward the boy. "My son, Nicolas, will give you a tour of the Apollo II as soon as all the passengers arrive."

I stood impatiently at the railing while the others climbed slowly up, and I had a hard time keeping my eyes off Nicolas Tombazi. He was wearing white shorts and a jacket, almost like a uniform. His dad looked Greek, but Nicolas looked like any California kid.

Miss Loring came up beside me and whispered, "Isn't Nicolas cute? I wish I were younger."

I was glad she wasn't.

We met the other 12 passengers. There was an Australian man, a Norwegian woman, a Japanese couple, a family of Germans, and the rest were Americans or Canadians. There weren't any other kids our age.

The captain introduced us to our tour guide, a young woman named Irene. She showed the adults around the yacht, while Nicolas took us kids on a tour.

"Here is a schedule that tells how long we'll be at each island, and dates and times for special island tours," Nicolas said. "Because of the storm, we weren't able to get more copies made." He held out a yellow paper. "I hope you three can share this one."

"Sure, we can," I said, taking it.

Yancey tried to grab it from me. "Give it to me," he said. "You'll lose it."

"I won't lose it." I wished my brother wouldn't make a big deal out of it in front of Nicolas. "I don't see why everybody automatically assumes I'll goof up."

Deanna and Yancey just looked at me.

"Okay, okay, so I do mess up sometimes. But I promise I'll take good care of the schedule," I said.

"Let's have a look around the Apollo II," Nicolas said.

He didn't even have much of an accent. I guess he learned American slang from people on the tours. He was easy to talk to and friendly. I liked him right off. You know how it is with some people you meet. Sometimes you just like them. Other times you know you'll never get along. I felt like I wanted to get to know Nicolas better.

I had only been half-listening as he explained about the yacht. I was wondering if he liked American rock music. "The Apollo II is 85 feet long," he was saying. "It has two diesel eng—"

"Why does it have engines" Yancey asked. "I thought this was a sailing ship." He sounded a little disappointed.

"Well, it is. But the winds are unpredictable. And we have to keep to a timetable."

"Oh, sure, that's right," Yancey said.

Nicolas showed us the salon-dining area. Next he took us below where there were several cabins. He opened a door to a rest room. He pointed to the toilet. "This is the only one that's working," he said. "It's a little hard to use." He pointed to a handle that looked like the gearshift on a sports car. "You have to really pull the handle to flush the toilet."

Then he took us up on deck. I looked out at the dark blue Aegean Sea. It was the same color as Nicolas' eyes. The sea was calm, and the air smelled tangy fresh. This was great.

I went over to Deanna who was leaning on the rail, still looking a little sick. "What do you think of him?" I asked.

"Who?" she asked in an uninterested voice.

"Nicolas," I whispered. "I'm glad your yacht was damag—I'm sorry, I don't mean that. But I'm glad we got to come on this tour."

"To tell you the truth," Deanna said, "I kind of wish we were touring the islands by bus!"

"I'm really sorry you got seasick. Is there anything I can do?"

"Yeah. Give me a new stomach."

Nicolas called to us. "We're going to a

37

taverna—a restaurant—now."

I was glad, because I was starving. I looked over at Deanna. She was swallowing hard and looking pretty green, as if eating wasn't exactly first on her list of things to do.

Everybody followed the captain down the gangplank. Nicolas joined Yancey, Deanna, and me, and the four of us brought up the rear.

As we were walking along the harbor to the restaurant, I saw a bearded man sitting at a table in an outdoor café. The setting sun gleamed on his mirrored glasses. He looked familiar. When he stood up, I knew who it was. He was the hulky guy at the airport who had gotten Sonia's autograph. For a minute I wondered if he had followed Sonia. I remembered a movie I'd seen where a fan followed and hassled a movie star, scaring her to death.

Then I laughed at myself. I was getting as bad as Yancey, always being suspicious of people.

Nicolas was telling us a little of the history of the island when I heard a funny smacking sound. "What's that?"

Nicolas motioned for us to follow him toward the docks. A bunch of kids, all the way from five or six years old to boys older than Nicolas were hitting rubbery-looking things against the rocks.

"What are they doing?" Deanna wanted to know.

"They're beating the boneless ones to tenderize them," Nicolas said.

We all looked confused.

"That's what we call squid and octopus," Nicolas explained.

Deanna made a face. "Ughh! You mean people *eat* them?"

"Yes, after they've been tenderized. They're one of our favorite foods," Nicolas told her. "You'll have to try them."

"Not me," I said. "I'll never get that awful sound out of my head."

I glanced at Deanna. She looked even sicker than before.

We had to hurry to catch up with the rest of the group. We followed them into the dark taverna. Inside, several bare wooden tables had been shoved together to hold all of us. Deanna sat on one side of me. Sonia took the chair at my other side. Yancey and Nicolas sat right across from us.

The captain said the lobster was really good, so that's what we all ordered. While we waited for our dinner, the captain told funny stories about some of the passengers he'd had over the years. I kept watching Nicolas. I could

39

tell he was proud of his father.

The lobsters finally came, and they were the biggest things I'd ever seen. It tasted okay, but I really liked the deep-fried, seafood stuff that was served on the side.

"What's this?" I asked Nicolas after I'd gobbled down half a dozen. "They're super."

"It's calimeri," he said. "Do you really like it?"

"It's great."

"It sure is," Yancey said. "Maybe we could open a fast-food calimeri stand back home."

"Is it fish or shrimp, or what?" Deanna asked.

Nicolas smiled. "Calimeri is our name for squid—you know, the boneless ones!"

"Squid!" Deanna and I yelled at the same time. I covered my mouth. All I could think of was the sound of the squid-whoppers.

"Nicolas, you rat, you asked your dad to order squid, didn't you?" I said.

He just gave me a devilish grin. I couldn't help smiling back. He had a weird sense of humor like I did.

"I know a place that sells wonderful desserts," Sonia whispered. "Maybe some chocolate cake would take the taste of squid out of your mouth."

"Actually, it didn't taste half-bad. It's just

the idea," I said.

"Let's sneak out anyway," Sonia whispered. "Just the two of us."

I glanced at Deanna and knew she'd heard Sonia's invitation. I really wanted to go, but I didn't want to hurt Deanna's feelings. "Thanks, but I'd better not," I told Sonia.

"Some other time, then," Sonia said, flashing her dazzling smile.

After dinner, the tour guide took us to our funny little hotel. The lobby was just a bare room with a desk. There was no TV and no couches or chairs.

"I'll leave you now," Irene, our tour guide, said. "Be sure to be at the boat by four in the morning, or we may have to leave without you."

"Four!" Yancey groaned. "I thought this was a vacation."

"We have a long trip ahead of us," she told him.

Deanna and I had a room together. Yancey had to room with the Australian man. I whispered to Yancey and Deanna, "I'm not sleepy yet. Let's go see what the town looks like."

"We have to get up too early," Deanna said.

"Let's just go for a few minutes. Yancey, how about you?" I knew if he went, Deanna would go along.

"Yeah, I guess I'll come along," he said. "I'll

41

meet you down here in 10 minutes."

Deanna and I carried our bags up the marble steps to a landing and then up some more stairs and through a narrow archway.

Our small room had bare, white walls, two narrow beds, a dresser, and two chairs. There was a balcony where we could look out at the sea. Purple flowers and ivy practically covered the railing. A full moon was just coming up over the hills behind the town.

"Isn't this just too incredible?" I asked. I gave Deanna a hug. "Thanks a million for asking Lance and me to come along."

"Oh, you know it wouldn't have been any fun without you two," she said. Then her face turned serious. "Kirstie, do you think we'll be friends even after we grow up and get married and don't live next door to each other anymore?"

"Well, sure. If we've made it through 14 years together, we can do 50 more—no problem." I frowned. "Why would you ask a question like that, anyway?"

"Oh, I don't know. I guess because I heard Miss Loring invite you to go someplace. I started thinking how we'll both meet new people and make new friends as we grow up..." Her voice trailed off.

"Come on, Deanna. I don't know about you,

but I have room in my heart for lots of friends. But you'll always be my best friend. Hey, what do you want us to do, cut our fingers and become blood sisters?" I asked, teasing her.

She laughed. "No, I get sick at the sight of blood—mine, anyhow. Come on. Let's go find Lance."

As we headed back downstairs, I asked, "What do you think of Nicolas? Isn't he just about the cutest guy you've ever seen?"

"Yeah, I guess he's all right—if you like those handsome, blond types." She pretended to yawn like she was bored to talk about handsome guys, and we both got the giggles.

We met Yancey in the lobby. Behind the hotel we followed a narrow stone street that led to rows of houses which were built up along the hillsides. In the moonlight the cube-shaped buildings were as white as sugar, like nothing I'd ever seen before. The houses were so close to the street that we could almost hear what people were saying inside—if we could have understood Greek. A cat jumped off a low balcony, and Deanna and I both let out a yell.

"There's somebody up ahead," Yancey said.

In the bright moonlight I could easily make out the figure of Jerry. "It's Mr. Burke," I said.

Just as I started to call out to him, a man

came out of the shadows and began talking to Jerry. We were too far away to hear what they were saying, though. We ducked back out of sight behind a wall.

The man was turned sideways to me, but I could see he had a beard and was wearing one of those black Greek fisherman's hats. I was sure it was the same man I'd seen earlier at the café by the harbor. Then he turned toward us. The moonlight reflected on his mirrored glasses, and I knew I was right.

"That guy was at the Athens airport getting Sonia's autograph," I whispered. "At least, that's what I thought he was doing. And then I saw him again when we first got off the yacht."

"I'll bet those two are up to something," Yancey said.

"Don't be a jerk," I said. "The man probably has something to do with the movie they're going to make."

"He looks more like a crook," Yancey said. "I mean, who wears sunglasses at night? Maybe they're moonglasses."

"Since when are you an expert on crooks or filmmakers?" I asked.

"Let's get out of here," Deanna whispered.

We moved quietly down the stone steps to the main street. "I didn't like that Burke guy from the beginning. I don't trust a guy who carries a cane with a poison dagger inside it."

I sighed. My brother was a hopeless case. "Well, I like both Jerry and Sonia a lot."

"You don't even know them," Deanna said in a sharp tone of voice.

"I know Sonia. We're fr—" I stopped, remembering what Deanna had said earlier about friends. Couldn't Deanna understand that a person can have lots of friends?

We headed back to the hotel. In our room, Deanna and I undressed quickly and climbed into our beds. "This mattress feels like it's full of sand," I said.

"Well, at least it's not moving, so I won't get seasick on it," Deanna answered.

The moon streamed through the glass doors of the balcony and made a line of silver across the beds. "Isn't Greece the most romantic place you've ever seen?" I asked.

She sighed. "I guess so. Kirstie, do you think your brother likes me?"

"Sure he does," I said sleepily.

She raised up on her elbow. "But did you see the way he looked at Miss Loring at the airport? He's never looked at me like that."

I gave a sigh of relief. Deanna was jealous of Sonia because of Yancey, not because of me. "That's because we all grew up together,"

I told her. "He knows you too well. But I'll bet on this trip he'll start seeing you in a different way. Grandma Lillian says Greece puts a romantic spell on you. So, maybe it'll put a spell on Lance."

"I hope so." She yawned loudly. "We'd better get to sleep, or we'll never be able to get up."

I think I fell asleep the minute I closed my eyes. When I heard the alarm clock go off, I felt like I'd only been asleep a few minutes. I couldn't get my eyes open. I must have fallen back to sleep, because suddenly Deanna was shaking me. "Kirstie, get up! We'll miss the boat if we don't hurry."

"Let me sleep just a few more minutes," I pleaded.

"No! Get up! It's already after 3:30. I'm going downstairs." She carried her suitcase out of the room and clunked down the hallway.

I couldn't believe it was already time to get up. I didn't want the boat to go off and leave me, so I jumped out of bed, threw on my clothes, and yanked at the doorknob. The darn door was stuck. I couldn't get it open.

"Help! Somebody, help!" I yelled. "I'm locked in!"

Four

I yanked and yanked on the door, but it just wouldn't open. I hurried out on to the balcony, leaned over the railing, and yelled, "Somebody, help me!"

"Kirstie!" Yancey was banging on my door. "You'd better get out here, or the yacht's going to leave without us."

I hurried back inside. "Lance, if I *could* get out, I would. The door's stuck."

I could hear him muttering. "There's nobody at the desk, but I'll see if I can find somebody in charge. Wait here!"

"Wait here? That's the dumbest thing you've ever said!" I shouted. "Where am I going to go?"

I got dressed fast and paced around the tiny room for what seemed like a long time. Finally, I heard someone at the door. A voice in Greek said something.

"Lance, is that you? What's going on?" I was getting pretty nervous by then.

"The manager can't get the door open, either," Yancey said. "It looks like he's going into the room next door."

"How's that going to help?" I asked.

"Beats me. I can't understand what he says. Boy, you've done it this time. You've pulled some stupid things, but this one tops them all."

A sound at the balcony startled me. I turned to see a man climbing over a connecting wall between our balcony and the one next door. He came through the balcony door and, without even looking at me, he tried to open the stuck door. But he couldn't get it open. He pointed to my bag and motioned for me to follow him out on to the balcony.

As I scrambled over the shoulder-high wall with my suitcase, one of my sandals came off and dropped back onto the balcony. I started to climb down to get it, but the man jerked an arm at me, and I figured I'd better follow him—with or without shoes.

I followed the man into the room next door to ours, and Yancy was waiting in the doorway.

"Kirstie, come on!" Yancey yelled. "We'll never make the boat in time!"

"I'm coming, I'm coming." I said.

Yancey grabbed my bag and began to run down the stairs to the lobby.

"Where is everybody?" I asked.

"They went ahead to the yacht to tell the captain not to leave without us."

I hobbled along after Yancey. When we got out onto the cobbled streets, I had to slow down. The full moon was bright, but I couldn't see the rocks. I kept stubbing my bare toes.

"Hurry up. We'll never make it in time," he said.

Gritting my teeth, I ran after him. Finally, we came to the little harbor. "The yacht's still there," I gasped, totally out of breath.

The captain, Nicolas, and half the passengers were waiting at the top of the gangplank. And believe me, there wasn't a happy face among them, except for Nicolas'. He was grinning at me. I looked down at myself—one bare foot, my blouse buttoned wrong. And I could imagine what my hair looked like. I was a mess! No wonder Nicolas was grinning.

As we came aboard, Deanna glared at me. "What did you do *this* time?"

"You sound just like my mother. I didn't do anything. The door to our room was stuck."

Yancey actually defended me—miracle of miracles! "Kirstie really was stuck in the

49

room," he said. "For once, it wasn't her fault."

"I'm afraid we probably won't get to Santorini in time to do much sightseeing today," the captain announced. "Because of the delay, we're a little behind schedule."

Nobody looked toward Yancey and me, but I knew everyone thought it was my fault. You'd have thought I'd personally glued the dumb door shut. I slunk down to the cabins below so I could get another pair of shoes from my bag and finish dressing.

I was trying to brush the tangles out of my hair when Sonia tapped on the door. I let her in. "Don't let the other passengers bother you," she said and put her arm around me.

"I just feel so dumb. I wish I'd never come on this trip."

"You don't really mean that, do you?"

"No. But things like this happen to me all the time. No matter what I do, something always goes wrong."

"Just laugh it off, Kirstie. So what if we miss some sightseeing?"

"Thanks. I only wish everybody felt like you do," I said. Sonia was the first person who really seemed to understand what it was like to be Kirstie.

I looked down at myself. "I must have looked like a stray cat."

She laughed. "Well, you did look as if you'd dressed in a hurry—and in the dark."

I sighed. "I saw Nicolas laughing at me."

"I don't blame you for being interested in him," she said.

"Uh, who says I'm interested in him?" I asked.

She smiled again. "Right. Who could be interested in a cute blond guy with gorgeous blue eyes. A girl would have to be crazy to even look at him," she said sarcastically.

I couldn't help smiling at that. "He'd never look at me—except to laugh." I touched my hair. "Look at my hair! It's a mess!"

"I can fix it up with my curling iron," Sonia said. "I'll get it out of my bag."

"Thanks," I said. "That would be great." Unbelievable! I just couldn't get over how nice Sonia was to me.

As she curled my hair she looked at my face. "I think maybe you need a little help with makeup. I'll tell you what," she said. "When we get to Santorini, you come to my room, and I'll make you look beautiful."

I didn't know how she was going to make an ordinary person like me look beautiful. But she was obviously the expert on being beautiful. "Thanks," I said. "I'd appreciate that."

When she finished with my hair, I looked

in the mirror. She had definitely done a great job fixing it.

"Now, let's go up on deck and watch the sun rise."

Most of the passengers were standing at the railing watching the sun come up. To the west, the huge moon was turning pale.

The sea looked dark and smooth except where the moon's rays made a strip of silver on the water. "It's beautiful," I whispered.

"There's something magical about Greece," Sonia said softly.

"That's what my grandma says."

As the sky turned rosy gold, Yancey started our video camera rolling. I noticed he kept it aimed more at Sonia than he did on the sunrise.

He was still taking pictures when Irene called us into the salon-dining area for a breakfast of juice and sweet rolls. After breakfast most of the passengers went on deck to sunbathe or read or just talk. Everyone was relaxed. Sonia was right. The world hadn't come to an end just because I'd made everybody late. I went over to Deanna to talk, but her eyes were closed. She was either asleep or was still mad at me. I didn't feel like lying in the sun so I went over to Yancey.

"Lance, do you want to do something?"

But he was listening to his portable tape recorder. He can never hear anything with the earplugs jammed in his ears. I picked up the video camera from beside his deck chair and started taking some videos. It was fun being able to move around and get action shots. It was like being a movie director. I headed for the salon. Nicolas was cleaning up the galley, and Irene was washing huge bunches of grapes and putting them in ice water.

I didn't look directly at Nicolas. "Do you mind if I take some pictures of you?" I asked Irene.

"I have to go read some things for the tour. Why don't you take some of Nicky?"

I tried to sound casual. "Sure, if you're not boo tizzy." I felt my face get hot with embarrassment. "I mean, too busy."

Nicolas didn't laugh or even smile. "Sure," he said. "I have a break now."

I noticed some pictures of him on the wall. In several shots he was wearing a bathing suit and holding up a medal. "Are you a swimmer?" I asked.

He shrugged. "I won a few races in Athens. It's no big deal."

Nicolas not only looked like a southern California kid, he talked like one, too. "I've never won a medal in my life," I said. "Wait.

I take that back. Lance and I won a ribbon for our twin worms in the pet parade when we were five."

We went up on deck. I got some good shots of Nicolas, and then we leaned over the railing and talked. He asked where I lived. When I told him I lived in southern California, he said that was where his mother came from.

"Then you're half American?" I asked.

He nodded. "She came to the island of Paros to study art and met my father who was a fisherman then. They got married and..."

"...lived happily ever after on a Greek island," I finished for him.

His face clouded, and he turned away. "No. She died when I was seven."

"Oh, I'm sorry." Why did I always have to say the wrong thing?

"It's all right. It's been a long time, and I have good memories of her."

"Well, that explains it. I wondered where you got your blond hair and blue eyes. You sure don't look Greek, Nicolas."

"I do sort of look like my mother, but lots of Greeks are blond," he answered. "And my friends call me Nicky."

"Have you ever been to America..., Nicky?"

"No, but it's always been my dream to go there."

"Well, I've always wanted to see Greece, and here I am. So, maybe you'll see America someday."

We talked for a while longer. It was really easy to talk to Nicky. I couldn't believe how many things we had in common. He liked rock music and old movies, chocolate, horseback riding, and, of course, swimming. And we both hated flies.

I was sorry when he had to go back to work. I could hardly wait to tell Deanna and Sonia about Nicky, about how nice he was. But they were both asleep in their deck chairs.

I went below to the restroom. I remembered how Nicky had said you had to pull the handle hard. Well, I did, but nothing happened.

Then I tugged on it really hard.

Nothing happened. So, I braced my foot against the door and yanked it as hard as I could.

The darn thing broke off in my hand!

Leaning against the door, I held up the handle to look at it. I didn't know whether to laugh or cry. Nicky had definitely said to pull it hard.

If you follow directions and do what you're told, things are supposed to work out right, aren't they?

Not if you're name is Kirstie Allen.

Five

IT took us two days to reach the island of Santorini, our first stop. We arrived at sunset on the Fourth of July. As the Apollo II sailed into the little harbor, Deanna and I looked up at the high cliffs of twisted rock. They were every shade of green, gray, yellow, and blue. Little buildings were perched way up at the top.

"The island is an extinct volcano of white marble," Irene said. "It blew up in 1500 B.C."

I took a look at the schedule. "I'm glad we'll have a couple of days here," I said as I put the schedule in my back pocket. "This place is neat."

The captain and Nicky stayed on the yacht. The rest of us rode mules up the steep zigzag steps to the town. My mule kept getting too close to the rock walls beside the path. I think he did it on purpose so I'd scrape my leg.

Irene started telling us about ghosts on the island. I wanted to hear what she was saying, but my stupid mule kept hanging back. I gave him a little nudge with my foot. That made him even grumpier, and he practically stopped.

I wanted to catch up, so I gave him a harder kick with my heel. He took off. The path was covered with what my grandmother calls donkey doo-doo. Guess where I ended up when that dumb donkey came screeching to a stop? I went right over the top of him and landed in a big pile of the grossest stuff you've ever seen! My favorite pink shorts were ruined, and that's an understatement!

"Are you all right?" Sonia called. "Do you need some help?"

I shook my head. I sat there for a minute.

We were close to the top, so I decided I'd walk the rest of the way—very carefully. The mule just walked up by himself. At the top, the others were waiting for me. Yancey was howling with laughter. Deanna was trying not to laugh, but she couldn't help it.

I just stared at them. "What are you laughing at?"

"Take a guess. Don't you know you should never kick a mule?" Yancey asked. Then he hee-hawed. I could have kicked him.

"I'm sorry," Deanna began, and then she broke into giggles. "I wish you could have seen yourself going over that mule's head into all that..." She had to stop because she was laughing so hard.

I just walked right by them, like I didn't have a care in the world. Although it's pretty hard to look like you don't have a care in the world when you're covered with mule manure.

Sonia came over to me. "You poor thing. Take a hot shower when you get to the hotel, and you'll feel better. I'm just glad you're not hurt."

"I think I'll become a comedian. I seem to be able to make people laugh," I said.

"Try not to let it bother you," she said. "Don't forget that I'm going to help you with your hair and makeup. Come to my room in about an hour and a half."

"Thanks. I'll be there."

When we checked in at the hotel, I noticed the clerk sniffing. I tried to hang back so he wouldn't notice me. As everybody was gathering in the lobby to go out to eat, Deanna came over to me. "I'm sorry I laughed," she said, and she was still laughing. "Do you want me to bring you something to eat?" she asked.

"Yeah, bring me a hamburger and fries," I said, knowing it would be easier to get take-out food on the moon than it would be here. "Bring me anything except some boneless ones."

They all left, and I went to our room. There wasn't any shower stall or bathtub, so I just put my filthy clothes on the tile floor and turned on the water. The water came out in a trickle. Great. I was going to smell like a sewer for the rest of the trip. Finally, the water came on enough for me to get clean and to wash my shorts and T-shirt.

I was drying my hair when Deanna came back from the restaurant. She brought me *souvlaki*, chunks of lamb on a stick, and something she called cheese pie. I was pretty hungry, and it tasted really good.

Deanna was bubbling. "Hey, what are you so happy about?" I asked.

"After we visit the archaeological dig tomorrow, Lance and I are going snorkeling with Nicolas. You're invited, too. And tonight we're going to play Scrabble." Her tone changed. "Lance said to ask you to play, but I know you don't like games."

I'd had some unenthusiastic invitations before, but this was the worst. I knew that Deanna wanted to have Yancey to herself. So, I said, "Sonia—I mean, Miss Loring—is going to help me with my hair and makeup tonight.

59

Who knows, when she gets through with me, maybe I'll look like a movie star."

"How come she's so nice to you?" Deanna asked. "Don't you thinks it's kind of weird that a famous person would help you do your hair and stuff like that?"

"No, it doesn't seem weird to me. She's really nice." I sighed.

When I finished eating, I didn't feel like sitting around, so I decided to go to Sonia's room. "I'll be back about 10:00," I told Deanna.

"Aren't you leaving too early?" she asked.

"Sonia won't mind."

Deanna had her back to me as she said softly, "You're always running off somewhere, always doing something."

"Do you want to come with me? I thought you wanted to play Scrabble with Lance."

"I do. But, oh, I don't know. You're making new friends, like Nicky and Sonia. Just forget it. You wouldn't understand."

I figured she was jealous that Sonia was nice to me. I was sorry if she felt left out. But it wasn't my fault if she was jealous over a silly thing like Sonia helping me look better.

"Well, have fun with Lance," I said, but she didn't answer. I left.

Sonia's room was on the second floor. I was about to knock, but I heard Jerry's voice, kind of loud, like he and Sonia were arguing.

"It's too dangerous to use a kid," he said.

"But she's perfect," Sonia said. "Kirstie's the girl-next-door type, and I don't think we could find anybody better."

They were talking about me! I could hardly keep from shouting. Maybe Sonia wanted me to be in their movie!

"Maybe so," Jerry was saying. "But let's wait until we get to Mykonos to decide."

Feeling a little embarrassed at eavesdropping, I quickly knocked. Sonia opened the door. "Oh, Kirstie, I wasn't expecting you yet. You're a little early."

"I'm sorry. I can come back later. I didn't mean to interrupt your business."

"No problem. Come on in. We're always talking business," she said, smiling.

I went in and sat down on a chair. I really wanted to let on that I knew they were thinking about using me in their movie. But I was afraid I might blow the whole thing.

Casually, I said, "It must be exciting to make a movie. I love to take pictures. Maybe I'll be a filmmaker someday." I turned to Jerry. "Are you going to use this island in your movie? Santorini would be good in a scary movie with ghosts and stuff like that."

"Well, uh, we haven't decided yet," he said.

"I just thought you might use those caves we saw on the cliff. I, uh, heard you say it would be dangerous."

Sonia and Jerry exchanged quick glances, and I was afraid I'd said too much. "You're right," Sonia said. "We were talking about how dangerous those cliffs are. We're afraid we'd never get our actors to climb up them."

"Oh, Lance and I climb mountains. Before Grandma Lillian broke her hip, she used to take us backpacking."

Again I was afraid I'd said too much. I didn't want them to think I was auditioning for a part.

Jerry went back to reading his newspaper. He looked at it for a little bit. Then, suddenly, he wadded it up and threw it into the wastebasket.

I had to laugh. He looked exactly like my dad. "Congress must have done something dumb. That's when my dad throws the paper into the trash."

"This is a Greek newspaper," he said. "About all I can make out are the headlines."

"Let's get started on you," Sonia said. "We have to be up early to catch the bus to the archaeological digs."

"I'd rather spend the day swimming and snorkeling with Nicky," I said to Sonia. "But

Mrs. Foley says we should learn some history on this trip."

"You'll like the digs, I think. Just remember not to pick up anything at the dig. It's against the law to take even a rock out of Greece."

I followed Sonia into the bathroom. "This has sure been one weird Fourth of July," I said. "There hasn't been even one firecracker or sparkler."

"You're having a good time, though, aren't you?" she asked.

"Oh, sure, I am. I just wish I'd stop having disasters."

"Don't feel bad. I used to be just like you. I had to learn to be more careful, move more slowly, and try to think ahead. My problem was that I couldn't wait. I wanted everything to happen right *now*."

"That's the way I feel, too. I want to do everything in the world."

"Just like your grandmother, right?" Sonia asked.

I nodded. "Nothing stops her."

"How old is she?" Sonia asked.

"She's 63."

"She's had 63 years to do all she's done. So relax, and don't take life in one gulp. You have years to do everything you want—just like your grandmother."

That's what Mom and Dad always said. Maybe they were right about that, after all. I just wish they would talk to me like an adult, the way Sonia did.

Sonia got out a large magnifying mirror so I could watch what she was doing. "Let's start with makeup," she said. "You're so young that you don't need makeup base, but use it for special occasions—like tomorrow. You can take this bottle with you. It's your shade." Next she got out some eye makeup.

"Mom doesn't let me use much of that," I said.

"Your mom's right. You want to use just enough to set off your brown eyes."

She showed me how to curl my hair and use hair spray to give it more body. The time went really fast. Sonia told me about her acting career, and I told her about school and things like that. After a while, I glanced at my watch. "It's after 10:00," I said. "Maybe I'd better get back to my room."

"Why don't you take the curling iron with you. I don't need it. And you want to look pretty for Nicolas tomorrow."

I blushed. "I kind of think he likes me."

"Well, why wouldn't he? You're a very pretty girl."

I had a feeling that Nicky wasn't the kind of guy who judged a girl just by her looks. But I checked myself in the mirror and decided it couldn't hurt to look my best. I mean, why take a chance, especially when I had Miss Sonia Loring, star of the movie *Terror at Midnight*, as my special beauty consultant?

I thanked her. As I was leaving, I said goodnight to Jerry. I noticed he had taken the wrinkled newspaper out of the wastebasket and was reading it again.

When I got back to my room, Deanna wasn't there. So I went down the hall to Mrs. Foley's room. She was dozing in her chair, and Yancey and Deanna were playing Scrabble.

"Who's winning?" I asked.

"Lance is, but he keeps trying to use those weird words in your special language. I don't think we should count them."

While Deanna was trying to think of a word, Yancey said to me, "I don't think you should hang out with those people."

"I'm not hanging out with them," I said. "Sonia was showing me how to do my hair and makeup."

"Kirstie, you're pretty enough just the way you—" Then he stopped when he realized he had almost given me a compliment. "I mean, who wants a sister who looks like a Barbie doll?"

"Well, for your information, they might ask me to be in their movie," I blurted out.

Yancey hooted. "And I'm going to be starting for the Los Angeles Lakers! You're as bad as Grandma Lillian about movie stars. Where did you get a dumb idea like that?"

"I overheard Sonia and Jerry talking about me. They haven't actually asked me yet, but she thinks I'm perfect," I explained. "Jerry thinks it's too dangerous because they're going to use the caves here in Santorini. Only, you can't say anything about it to anybody. I'm not supposed to know."

Yancey shook his head. "I still don't believe it. And Mom and Dad would never let you do it."

"What about school?" Deanna asked. "And what about—"

"I thought you'd both be happy for me," I said, cutting her off. "You're just jealous."

I charged out of the room and slammed the door.

But in the hall, all my anger faded away. I just felt bad that my own brother and best friend didn't want me to get the chance to do something fabulous.

Six

THE next morning in our room I spent an hour curling my hair with Sonia's curling iron and using makeup the way she'd shown me.

"I don't know why you're going to all that trouble," Deanna said. "We're going swimming after we get back from the dig."

"I just want to look nice," I said.

"You want to look good for *Nicolas*," she teased.

"All right, I want to look good for *Nicky*. He told me his friends call him Nicky." I sighed. "I'll bet he has a lot of friends—especially girl-friends."

"Your hair does look great," Deanna said, as if she were trying to make me feel good. "You should wear it that way all the time."

"Hey, if you want me to, I'll ask Sonia to show you how to look glamorous—you know, so Lance might notice."

"Do you think she would?"

"Sure. She helped me, and you're my friend." I unplugged the curling iron. "Well, I'm ready. Let's go eat."

"What time does the schedule say we're supposed to meet at the bus?" Deanna asked.

"We're supposed to be there at 9:30, I think."

"You *think*? Let me see the schedule," Deanna said.

I started rummaging through my things, and then I remembered I'd had the schedule in my pink shorts—the pink shorts that were involved in that accident with the donkey you-know-what. "I must have thrown it away."

"Oh, no! Kirstie Allen, I think you'd lose your head if it wasn't attached."

"It was in the pocket of my shorts, and my shorts were a mess. I don't know what happened to the schedule."

Deanna looked disgusted.

"Well, it wasn't my fault that the stupid mule threw me. Anyway, what's the big deal?" I grabbed the video camera. "Mrs. Foley has a schedule. Let's get going."

We hurried down to the hotel restaurant and looked around. "I don't see Lance or Mrs. Foley or any of our tour group. I guess I was wrong about the time," I said.

"Come on! Maybe we can catch them at the bus," Deanna said.

We dashed out. The bus was supposed to pick us up at the end of the street. We got there just in time to see the bus drive away, headed for the digs.

"Well," I said, "I didn't really want to go, anyway. Let's eat breakfast. I'm starving."

"As usual," Deanna said.

After we ate breakfast, we took a walk around the town. Deanna seemed to be in a better mood, too.

"Everything—the houses, the trees, the people—all looks so foreign," I said.

"That's not so strange since we're so far from home."

"Home...gosh, I haven't even thought of home lately. Let's get some postcards. I want to send one to Mom and Dad, Grandma Lillian, and to some of our friends."

We bought cards and looked in the little shops. After we'd wandered around for a while taking video pictures, we were both thirsty. We found a little café where the waiter didn't speak any English.

"I think I'm going to ask Nicky to teach me some Greek," I said. "I wonder how you say cola in Greek."

Deanna got out her little Greek-English dictionary. "I can't find anything for cola. Oh, here, I can pronounce this." "Lehmonahdah," she said to the waiter. "At least it sounds like lemonade," she said to me after the waiter left.

I was looking around, watching the people. Then I saw him. I was sure it was the same man we'd seen with Jerry.

"Don't be obvious," I said. "But turn around, and look at the man over there."

Deanna bent down like she was tying her shoe. "Oh," she gasped. "It's him!"

I picked up the camera and began taking pictures of Deanna, but I turned the camera so it would also get a shot of the man. Then we gulped down our drinks, paid, and got out of there fast. We practically ran back to the hotel.

Out of breath, we sank down in chairs in the lobby. "What do you think's going on?" Deanna asked. "How come that guy keeps showing up?"

Sitting safely in the hotel, I was beginning to feel a little silly for taking all those pictures of the strange man. "He's probably a tourist. After all, a lot of the tours go to the same islands. Or, maybe he's in business with Jerry. Maybe he's helping Jerry and Sonia

70

look for good places to make their movie."

"I guess that could be why he's here," Deanna said. "I kind of wish my mom and dad were here, though. They'd know what to do."

"My dad would say I was letting my imagination run away."

While we waited for the others to come back from the dig, I got out my postcards and started writing to Mom and Dad and Grandma. There was a lot that I wanted to tell them, but my mind kept coming back to the man in the mirrored sunglasses. I probably wouldn't have given him a second thought if Yancey hadn't talked about what a suspicious character he was. When was I going to stop listening to my dumb brother?

I hadn't even finished writing out one card by the time the tour bus got back. I looked for Sonia and Jerry. "Weren't Miss Loring and Mr. Burke with you?" I asked Mrs. Foley.

"No, they weren't. I thought you two girls must have been with them. Now, I don't want you to do this again, do you hear?"

Deanna and I nodded.

"I don't want you wandering around alone. I'm going upstairs to lie down. Don't leave for the yacht without telling me."

"We promise we won't," I said. I knew it was hard for Mrs. Foley to discipline us, even though we deserved it. She was just too nice!

Yancey was pretty excited. "You guys should have seen the digs," he said. "When the volcano erupted, ashes covered up a whole town. They think at least 30,000 people lived there. Boy, they even had three-story buildings way back then, and bathtubs, and everything. If I don't make it in basketball, I think I'll become an archaeologist."

When he finally slowed down, Deanna said, "You should have been with us. We saw—"

"We saw some of the town," I said, breaking in. I didn't want Yancey to know about the guy with the sunglasses. He'd want to go hunt the guy down, and I didn't want to miss the chance to go swimming with Nicky. "Let's get some lunch before we go to the yacht," I said before Deanna could say anything about the man in the sunglasses.

After we ate, we put on bathing suits under our clothes. We stopped to tell Mrs. Foley we'd be back by 4:00, and then we took off for the yacht. Unfortunately, the only way to get there was to walk down the same path we'd come up. Believe me, I was very careful of where I stepped.

Nicky and his dad met us with a small rowboat and the snorkeling gear. "Now, you kids be careful," the captain said. "You do exactly what Nicolas tells you. He knows these waters better than a fish does."

We rowed to a little cove and pulled the boat ashore. We stashed our clothes on some rocks, and in our bathing suits we waded into the beautiful green water.

"This is great, Nick," Yancey said. "Do you usually do this with people on the tour?"

Nicky glanced at me, and then he said. "No. My father wasn't very happy about it, but he knows I don't get to be with kids my own age much." He changed the subject. "Come on, let's swim along the coastline."

The three of us were pretty good swimmers, but Nicky was incredible. "Boy, Nick, you ought to be in the Olympics," Yancey told him.

"That takes special coaching," Nicky said, sounding a little sad.

"So, come to southern California," said Yancey. "We have great coaches there."

"Lance is right," I put in. "Lots of kids from other countries train in America."

"That takes money," said Nick. "We don't have that kind of money." The way he said it made me think he didn't want to talk about it.

We put on our masks, swim fins, and snorkels. We explored the bottom of the sea and watched the fish for a while. Then we swam back to the beach to rest and talk. Nicky wanted to know what our school was like in California and whether every kid had a car—and a million other things.

"What about you?" Deanna asked Nicky. "What do you do in the winter?"

"I go to school, and on weekends I work on our fishing boat."

I noticed he was wearing a chain with a tiny silver dolphin on it. Back home I'd think it was weird for a guy to wear a necklace. But on Nicky, and in Greece, it seemed just right. "I really like your dolphin. Is it a good luck charm?" I asked him.

He touched the dolphin. "Sort of. There are old Greek legends about the dolphin."

We talked and talked. I decided then and there I wouldn't mind living in Greece forever.

"I'm getting too warm," Nicky said, standing up. "Who wants to get back in the water?"

I jumped up. "I do. I'm getting burned in this sun."

Yancey and Deanna said they'd wait a while. As Nicky and I waded out into the water and put on our masks, he asked me if I'd like to swim to a grotto. I didn't know what a grotto was, but I said yes before he could change his mind.

As we swam underwater for a short distance, the water turned from green to a deep purplish blue. We came out in a large cave and sat on some rocks to rest. In the silvery-blue light, I saw little sea creatures scurrying away from us.

"Oh, Nicky, this is beautiful. I feel as if we're in some underground world."

He smiled. "I was hoping you'd like it. It's a special place I come to be by myself. I've never shown it to anyone else."

"I have a secret place at home, too. It's out in a field under an orange tree. Sometimes I lie down in the yellow and orange wildflowers and just look up at the sky. Nobody can see me, and I always feel as if I'm the only person in the world. I've never even told my brother about it."

Nicky looked around the cave. "This place makes me feel happy and sad at the same time. Isn't that crazy?"

I shook my head. "No, it's not crazy. You know, Nicky, I've never told anybody this. Sometimes when I'm in my secret spot, I just start crying. I mean, I don't feel bad or anything, but there I am crying."

"I think I understand," he said.

We didn't say anything for a while, and then he turned to me. "Do you think you'll ever come back to Greece again?"

"Oh, I hope so. I want to see every single island."

Nicky laughed. "You'd better plan to stay a long time then. There are about 3,000 islands!"

I knew I shouldn't say anything about the movie I might be in, but I couldn't help it. "I think I might be coming back to Santorini. Miss Loring and Mr. Burke are thinking about putting me in a movie they're going to make."

"That would be great if you could come back," Nicky said.

"I never thought about being an actress, but I think I'd be good at it. But don't tell anybody," I said quickly. "Nothing's been settled yet. Anyway, Lance and Deanna laughed at the idea."

"Well, I'm not laughing. I bet you'll make a good whatever you want to be. You're different from a lot of the girls who come on the tours."

"Is that good or bad?"

"To me, that's good. I don't know why, but I can talk to you. I usually get nervous around girls, especially American girls."

That surprised me. How could anybody like him be nervous around girls? "I guess it's easy for me to talk to guys because of my brother," I said. "We used to talk a lot, but we don't talk that much anymore. Somehow, as we got older, we just grew apart. I'm into stuff at school, and he's more interested in soccer and basketball."

"Lots of American basketball players come here to play," Nicky said.

That got me thinking about Nicky and swimming coaches. "You know, Deanna's family has had exchange students from England and Germany live at their house for the school year. Why don't I talk to Mr. Asbury about you? Maybe you could come stay with them. You could go to our school and get some good coaching."

"Oh, I don't even know Mr. Asbury. And, besides, my dad needs me here." Then he sighed. "But it would be incredible if I could go to California."

"It wouldn't hurt to ask. I bet—"

"Kirstie! Nick!" a voice broke into my speech.

Faintly, we could hear Yancey calling us.

"They must be worried," Nicky said. "We'd better go."

"Maybe you're right." I took one last look at Nicky's grotto. I didn't want anyone else to share it—not even my brother or my best friend.

Seven

THE next morning we continued with the tour. Although I was kind of sorry to leave Santorini, I was anxious to get to Mykonos. I wanted to find out if Sonia and Jerry had decided to put me in their movie.

Since I had become so interested in making movies, I took videos of everything. During the next three days, I got to know Nicky better. Whenever he had a chance, he showed Yancey, Deanna, and me around each island we visited. He taught me how to speak a little Greek. I taught him a few words of our secret twin language. Nicky and I really understood each other. Even though he's Greek, and I'm American, it was no problem. It's never been like that before with any other guy.

As we were heading for Mykonos, I was taking pictures of flying fish. Deanna came up to me, and I turned the camera on her.

"No, don't," she said. "I'm a mess."

"You look fine to me."

"Hey, you know what I just remembered? You never did ask Sonia to help me look glamorous," Deanna said.

"I did ask her a couple of times. But she said she was busy and would do it later."

"Well, she's not busy now." Deanna nodded to where Sonia was lying in a deck chair.

"Maybe she's asleep," I answered.

"I don't get you," Deanna said. "You act like you don't want anybody else to even talk to her."

"That's not it at all." But as I said it, I wondered if maybe Deanna was right. I felt pretty special that Sonia singled me out to be her friend. But I said, "Okay, come on. I'll go ask her right now."

As our shadows fell across her face, Sonia sat up and smiled at us. "I'm sorry if we woke you up," I said.

"It's okay. I was just lying here. Instead of a couch potato, I think I could easily become a deck chair potato. What's up, girls?"

"I just wondered if you'd have time now to help Deanna learn how to put on makeup. She'd like to look glamorous."

"I could never be beautiful like you are, Miss Loring," Deanna said quickly, "but..."

"She wants my brother to really look at her," I whispered.

"Kirstie!" Deanna shrieked.

"It's true," I said. "We all grew up together, and he thinks of her more as a sister."

"I think I understand," Sonia said. "Come on, Deanna. We'll see what we can do."

We went below to the cabins. Deanna went to Sonia's room, and I went to our room to put away the camera and to get a note pad and pencil. I wanted to tell Grandma all about Sonia and the movie, and even about Nicky.

Then I went back up to the salon to write my letter.

Dear Grandma Lillian:

This is our eighth day in Greece. The time is going too fast. I really wish you were here! We haven't been on the Asburys' yacht yet because it was damaged in a storm, but this tour is fantastic. Everything you told me about Greece is true.

Of course, I've had my usual problems, especially with toilets. First, I broke the handle off the one on the yacht. Then yesterday we were in a taverna, and I had to use the restroom. I didn't notice the curved metal spout at the back of the toilet, and when I leaned over to flush it, water poured out of the spout. I mean, talk about getting soaked! When I came out, everybody was laughing. They all think I'm funny. In fact, the other people on the tour keep asking me what new messes I've gotten myself into!

I don't mind, though. If we hadn't come on this tour, I'd never have met the captain's son, Nicky. Grandma, he's so nice. We like all the same things, and he really listens to me. I know you'd like him, too.

I stared out the window for a minute, remembering Nicky's secret grotto. Then I told her all about his swimming.

And if I hadn't come on this tour, I wouldn't have met Sonia Loring, the actress. I got her autograph for you. Remember, she was in Terror at Midnight. *She says she used to be like me—always getting into trouble. I'm going to try to be just like her. Maybe then Mom and Dad will believe me when I say I'm trying to be a responsible person.*

You'll love this, Grandma. Sonia and her husband Jerry are going to make a movie, and I think they're going to ask me to be in it! Can you believe it—me, Kirstie Allen, in a movie!

Oh, Grandma, I hope your hip is okay so you can come back to Greece with me. But

*don't tell Mom and Dad about the movie until
I get home. Maybe you can help me convince
them that it wouldn't hurt if I missed some
school to be in a movie.*

I had a whole lot more to write about, but
Irene came into the salon to tell me we were
coming into Mykonos. I went below to get the
video camera and poked my head into the
cabin to see how Deanna and Sonia were
doing.

"Wow! You look great," I said. "You look at
least 16 years old."

"Do I really?" Deanna asked.

"If my stupid brother doesn't notice you
now, he's blind."

Deanna looked at herself in the mirror and
giggled. I could tell she was excited. "I used
to think I'd have to look like Magic Johnson
to get Lance to look at me," she said.

"Did you two know we're coming into
Mykonos?" I asked. "I'm going up on deck to
take some pictures—if I haven't run out of
film."

"I'll be up in a minute," Deanna said. "I can't
wait for Lance to see me."

"I think you should take off the makeup,"
Sonia told her. "I was just showing you how

to do it for nighttime."

Deanna looked disappointed.

"Let me at least tone it down a bit," Sonia said.

"I'll see you up on deck," I told them. I got the camera, checked the tape, and went topside, as Nicky called it. I began taking videos of Mykonos harbor. It was full of small boats and three large cruise ships.

When Deanna came up, I called to Yancey, pretending I was having trouble with the camera. "Hey, Lance, would you come over here and help me?"

He turned around, got a look at Deanna, and his mouth fell open.

"Close your mouth," I whispered to him. "You look like a guppy."

He didn't say anything to Deanna. But as he fiddled with the camera, he kept sneaking looks at her.

"I think it's working," I whispered to Deanna a little later.

"Thanks for asking Sonia to help me. You know, she likes you," Deanna said. "She told me you remind her of her little sister Janie."

"Yeah, I told you that. Only her name was Jeanie."

"I sure thought she said Janie, but maybe I heard wrong," Deanna added.

"All right, everybody, gather up all your luggage," Irene said. "We'll be staying in Mykonos for four days."

She took us to our hotel near a beach. Cats were everywhere. It was creepy. I bet there wasn't a mouse on the whole island.

Deanna and I were tired and went to bed early that night. During the night, the screeching of cats woke me up. I heard Deanna stirring. "Are you awake?" I whispered.

"How can anybody sleep with all that noise?"

We talked for a few minutes about what we were going to do the next day. "I want to get some presents for Mom and Dad and Grandma Lillian."

"Do you think Lance would like one of those black fisherman's hats for a Christmas present?" she asked.

"Sure," I said. I was thinking about Sonia and Jerry. "I can't wait to find out about the movie," I said.

"You're sure getting your hopes up over this thing," Deanna said. "I mean, why would they pick someone like you, without any experience? You've never even been in drama club."

"They said they wanted a girl-next-door type. I guess that's me."

"Well, I hope they do ask you. Now, let's

try to get some sleep."

As I drifted off to sleep, I was wondering if Sonia and Jerry would consider using a Greek-American boy in their movie.

* * * * *

Deanna and I both slept late. A knock on the door woke us up. "Just a minute," I called. I scrambled out of bed and opened the door just wide enough to poke my head out.

"Oh, come on in, Sonia. I thought it was my brother. Deanna and I didn't get much sleep. Those carned dats—I mean, darned cats— woke us up last night."

I was babbling and could hardly hide my excitement. This was it. I was about to become a movie star! I turned to give Deanna a big I-told-you-so smile.

"I'm sorry I woke you up. I thought you'd be awake by now." Sonia handed me a small plastic bag. "I just stopped by to give you a little present."

I didn't know what to say. "You brought me a present? It's not my birthday or anything."

"It's just a little gift from Jerry and me."

I opened the bag to find a string of blue beads about the size of large marbles. Each one was different, painted with designs in

85

blue, green, pink, and yellow. "I love them," I said. "Thank you, Sonia."

"They're called worry beads."

Deanna laughed. "Worry beads?"

"Greek people click the beads together whenever they're nervous. I hope these bring you much luck. And be sure you don't get them near heat, or the paint will crack."

"I'll be careful," I said.

"My little sister Janie would have loved these," she said softly. "I'm glad you do, too."

Now it was Deanna's turn to give me an I-told-you-so smirk.

But I could have sworn Sonia had said Jeanie before.

I held the beads close. "I'll keep them forever."

"I almost forgot. Could I have your address and phone number?" Sonia asked. "I don't want us to lose track of each other."

I wrote down my phone number and address.

"I'll call you, and we can meet in Hollywood. How would you like to visit a movie set?" Sonia asked.

"Are you kidding? I'd *love* it," I said, nearly choking with excitement. "Does this mean I'm going to get a part in your movie?"

She turned quickly and stared at me for a

moment. I wished I hadn't mentioned it. "I—uh—heard you tell Jerry you wanted to use me because I was the girl-next-door type."

"Oh, well, we haven't made any final decisions on that. But I think it's very likely. I didn't say anything to you because I didn't want you to get your hopes up and then be disappointed if everything didn't work out. But that's the reason I wanted your address and phone number. I have a hunch you'll be hearing from me very soon."

I felt like I was floating. Who wouldn't be after hearing all that?

After Sonia left, I set the beads on the dresser.

"Come on," Deanna said. "Let's go eat breakfast. I'm starved."

"I'm too excited to eat. Did you hear what Sonia said? She thinks it's *very likely* that they'll ask me."

During breakfast, I went on about my new career. Mrs. Foley was sitting with us for breakfast. "I wonder if Mom will let me take acting lessons. I've heard they have tutors for kids who are in movies," I said.

"Do you think we could talk about something else?" Deanna asked.

"Deanna!" Mrs. Foley said. "Don't be rude. Naturally, Kirstie's excited."

"I'm sorry," Deanna said to me. "But you're going on and on about it."

"Maybe they'll need another girl as an extra," I said. "I'll ask if they can use you."

"Thanks. I'm not interested."

"Okay, I'll shut up about it." I couldn't understand why Deanna wasn't happy for me. I would have been happy for her.

During the day, we went sightseeing and shopping. We had to hurry back to our rooms to get dressed in our best clothes to go see Greek dancers that evening. Deanna was ready before I was. "How much longer are you going to be?" she asked. "You're usually standing at the door waiting impatiently."

"I know. Sonia said I should try to slow down. She said I wouldn't get into so much trouble if I didn't do everything in such a hurry. Did you notice I was the last one done eating this morning?"

"Now, I suppose you'll be late for everything, if Sonia says it's a good idea," Deanna said in a grumpy voice.

I had finished putting on makeup the way Sonia had taught me, but my hair was a mess from the shower. "I want to curl my hair," I said. "I'll be another half hour, at least."

"I wish you'd stop doing everything that woman tells you to do. If she told you to jump

88

off the mast of the Apollo II, you'd probably do it," she said. "I'll just meet you downstairs."

I plugged in Sonia's curling iron and set it on the dresser. While I was waiting for the iron to heat up, I thought about what Deanna had said. You'd think she'd be glad that I listened to Sonia. It was like she wanted me to stay the same old klutzy way, always messing things up and getting into trouble. Didn't she understand that people have to change and grow up?

I started to curl my hair and remembered that I needed the hair spray. The can wasn't on the dresser or in the bathroom. I figured Deanna must have used it up, so I went across the hall and borrowed Mrs. Foley's. When I came back into our room I smelled something burning. I rushed over to the dresser.

"Oh, no!" I cried.

The curling iron had fallen off its little stand and had landed on the string of beads. This was exactly what Sonia had warned me about not doing!

I looked more closely at the beads. Not only had the paint cracked on two of the beads, but they had come apart. Then I saw it. I couldn't believe my eyes. I just stood there staring at them. Inside each broken bead was a huge diamond!

Eight

I just stood there with a million questions running through my head. Diamonds! How could diamonds get inside the beads?

I snapped out of it and realized the iron was burning the dresser. I pulled the plug and put the iron back on its stand, and then I checked out the unsplit beads more closely. Each one looked as if it had been made in two parts and then glued together.

I was holding the diamonds up to the light when I heard a key in the door.

Deanna! I didn't want anybody to know about the diamonds until I'd had a chance to talk to Sonia. Without even thinking, I dropped them into the bottle of makeup base that I'd left open.

Deanna poked her head in. "Aren't you ready yet? Everybody's downstairs."

I put my hand over my forehead. "Uh, I'm

feeling kind of sick," I lied. "I think I better just go to bed."

She started to come in. "Hey, I'm sorry. Is there anything I can do?"

"No, you go on. Have a good time with the others. I just need to lie down. I'll be fine."

"Are you sure?" she asked, still hesitating. "I hate to leave you alone."

"Don't worry about it. I'll feel worse if I know I'm spoiling your fun. Really, I'm just tired. I'm probably coming down with a cold."

"Okay, but I won't stay late."

"Oh, by the way," I said casually, "Was Sonia downstairs?"

Deanna gave me a disgusted look. "I don't know. It's not my turn to watch her. I have to go, or they'll leave without me. See you later."

When she finally closed the door, I breathed a big sigh of relief. I hurried to the door and checked the lock. What if the person who'd put the diamonds in the worry beads knew I had them? What if they came after the diamonds? I wished there was a chain on the door, but there was only one of those locks where you push in the button on the knob.

I went back to the dresser and picked up the makeup bottle. I'd thought the diamonds would sink to the bottom, but they were right on top of the makeup. I shook the bottle, and the diamonds disappeared into the pink stuff.

Next, I took the two broken beads off the cord and hid them inside one of my shoes. The room was hot. I opened the door to the balcony and went out. The breeze felt good. Our room was on the third floor, and the balconies weren't connected like in the other hotel. I thought it was safe to leave the balcony door open.

The rest of the evening dragged by. I wished I were at the taverna dancing and learning the Greek dances. I wished the room had a TV. I wished I had Yancey's radio. I even wished I had Mrs. Foley's cards so I could play solitaire. All I had were a bunch of diamonds that I wished I'd never seen!

I almost went nuts waiting for everybody to come back from the taverna. Every time the plumbing gurgled or a cat yowled outside, I nearly jumped out of my skin. My eyes kept going back to the worry beads on the dresser. They were worry beads all right. I'd never been so worried in my life.

After what seemed like a million years, I heard the key in the lock. "Is that you, Deanna?"

"Yes, it's me," she said in a loud whisper as she came in. "Who did you think it was—a burglar?"

I tried to laugh, but I sounded more like a hysterical chimpanzee. She gave me a sharp look. "Are you okay? I think there must be something going around. Mrs. Foley left the taverna early because she wasn't feeling well." She glanced at the unrumpled beds. "I thought you were going to rest."

"I did, but I couldn't sleep."

She brushed back her hair. "It's really getting windy outside. And speaking of wind, Nicky invited you and Lance and me to go see the windmills of Mykonos tomorrow. I hope you'll feel okay tomorrow."

"I'll be fine. Did you have a good time?"

"It was great." Her face was all pink with excitement. "You should have seen the dancers. Lance and I even joined in on one of the dances—you know, the one where everybody links arms and they all kick together. It's the best time I've ever had and—" She gave me a silly grin. "Lance said I looked pretty tonight. He's never said that."

"Did—uh—did Sonia dance, too?"

"I don't think so. She and Jerry left early." As she took off her bracelet and set it on the dresser, she started to pick up the string of worry beads.

"Don't touch those!" I screeched.

"Well, *pardon* me."

"I'm sorry," I said, trying desperately to think up a good excuse why she shouldn't touch the beads. "I, uh, accidentally knocked the curling iron on one of the beads, and it cracked the paint. I'm afraid it'll come off."

I hurried to the dresser and picked up the iron. "See, it's got paint on it. That's why I asked about Sonia. I think I should take this to her right now."

"You're lying."

"What do you mean I'm—I'm lying? You can see the baint on the peads."

"I can see the paint on the beads," she said impatiently. "But that's not why you want to see your *dear* Sonia. You know what? I'm sick of hearing about her and her dumb movie."

"I thought you liked her, Deanna," I said, trying to keep from getting angry. "She helped you fix yourself up, remember?"

"She's okay, but you pay more attention to her than you do to me. You don't grow up with someone, tell each other secrets, and then just ignore her! Who asked you on this trip, anyhow?"

"Deanna..." I began.

"You'll be going off making movies, and you won't be going to school. And we'll never be friends again." She looked like she was about to cry.

"We'll always be friends, Deanna," I told her. "You know what Sonia asked me? She asked if I had room in my heart for another friend. Isn't that beautiful?"

"No, it's sickening." Deanna picked up the string of worry beads and then dropped them back on the dresser with a loud clatter.

I shut my eyes, afraid another bead would come apart.

"There! I touched your precious beads!" She grabbed her bag and headed for the door.

"Where are you going?" I demanded. "Stop acting like a little kid."

"I'm going to sleep in Mrs. Foley's room for the rest of the trip."

"Go ahead!" I shouted. "See if I care!"

The slam of the door seemed to echo in my ears. Ever since we were little kids we'd been having these stupid arguments, but this time I felt really bad about it. Maybe I had been talking too much about Sonia and the movie. But couldn't Deanna understand that she was still my best friend?

After a few minutes, when I was sure Deanna wasn't coming back, I put the beads in the plastic bag Sonia gave me. I took the bag and the bottle with the diamonds up the stairs to Sonia's room. I guess I should have gone right to Mrs. Foley with them, but I wanted to talk to Sonia first.

I knocked several times, but she didn't answer. I'd just have to wait until morning. I walked slowly back downstairs. Back in my room, I got ready for bed. I put the bottle with the diamonds on the table beside the bed where I could reach them. I put the plastic bag in the top drawer of my dresser.

I lay awake for a long time, wondering if the owner of the diamonds was lurking out there in the dark. I kept turning on the light and opening the bottle to see if the diamonds had floated to the top. They hadn't.

Finally, I fell asleep. I had an awful dream. *A man was following me. I felt a knife in my back. "Give me my diamonds, or you'll never see your family again!" the man shouted. I jerked away from him*, and I hit the table with my arm. I woke up in a sweat.

My nightgown felt damp and sticky, and so did the edge of the sheet. I switched on the light and saw the bottle of makeup on the bed. I must have knocked the bottle off the nightstand when I was dreaming. I hadn't put the lid on tightly. I was covered with the pink stuff.

I checked to see if the diamonds were safe. There was still enough makeup to cover them. Right then I wanted to throw the things off the balcony and let someone else worry about the awful worry beads.

I dug another nightgown out of my bag and went into the bathroom to take a shower. There was no tub or shower—just a floor with a drain. The water splashed all over everything, even the towels hanging on the rack. My nightgown was soaked.

As I was trying to dry myself with the damp towel, I suddenly felt water on my feet. I looked down. Instead of the water going down the big drain in the center of the bathroom, it was rising around my feet and getting all over the place.

Turning off the water as tight as I could and wrapping the towel around me, I sloshed my way to the door. I decided to run across the hall to Mrs. Foley's room before the water got any higher. I didn't care if Deanna was still angry with me. I had to get help.

I peeked into the hall to make sure nobody was in sight. The coast was clear. Just as I stepped out, I heard footsteps coming up the stairs. I turned to go back inside, but a gust of wind from the open balcony slammed the door shut.

There I was, standing in the hall in the middle of the night wearing a towel. This time I was locked *out* of the room!

Nine

"WHY me?" I groaned. How was I supposed to know the wind would blow the door shut?

The footsteps were coming closer. I leaned against the door, trying to look invisible. Then I saw that it was Sonia, although I hardly recognized her. She was wearing navy blue slacks, a turtleneck sweater, and running shoes. Her hair was hidden by a hat.

"Boy, am I ever glad to see you," I said.

She was surprised to see me standing there like that.

"Kirstie," she said. "What in the world are you doing out here like that?"

"I'm locked out. The drain's plugged, and my room is probably flooded by now. And there's nobody at the desk."

"Where's Deanna? Can't you wake her up?"

"Uh, we had a fight. She's sleeping in Mrs.

Foley's room. I don't want to bother them," I said. "Mrs. Foley's not feeling very well."

Sonia tried the door, rattling the knob. "Take my key. Go to my room, and I'll go get Jerry. He'll be able to open the door."

"I'd better wait here," I said, remembering the diamonds sitting on the table. I didn't want Jerry to find them before I had a chance to tell Sonia.

The floor was cold on my bare feet. Sonia saw me shivering. "No, you're freezing out here in the hall," she said. "You go to my room. I'll be right back."

I walked to her room. I went in and sat on a wooden chair so I wouldn't get anything wet. I noticed her bags were sitting by the door, as if she was planning to leave right away.

After a while, I heard a tap on the door. "It's me," Sonia said. I let her in.

"Jerry's in your room now. I'm sure he can fix everything. Now, young lady, you go take a hot shower before you freeze to death."

After the shower, Sonia gave me one of her nightgowns to wear.

I nodded toward the suitcases. "Are you leaving the tour?"

"Oh, Jerry and I thought we might fly back to Santorini."

"Then you've decided to use that island for

your new movie?"

"It's not final," she said. "I'd better go see how Jerry's doing."

"Sonia, wait. I need to talk to you first. Something pretty weird is going on."

She looked up quickly. "What do you mean—weird?"

"Well, you know the beads you gave me?"

"Yes. What about them?"

"I was using your curling iron, and I know you said not to get the beads near heat because the paint would crack—" I stopped.

"Well, go on."

"The iron fell over onto the beads, and two of them broke open. You won't believe this, but there was a diamond in each one of the beads," I said all in one breath.

"What!"

"Honest. Well, at least they look like diamonds."

"Where are they now?" she asked sharply. "I hope you didn't leave them lying around."

"No, I hid them in the bottle of makeup base you let me use. How do you think the diamonds got in the beads?"

"I have no idea," she said slowly. "You're right, though. It is weird."

"Sonia, I'm scared. What if the person who put them in the beads knows I have them? If this was like on TV, I'd be found in an alley with my head bashed in."

I jumped when Sonia put her arm around me. "Don't worry, Kirstie. I won't let anything happen to you." It felt good to have someone else know about the diamonds.

"I wonder if somebody is trying to use me to smuggle jewels," Sonia said.

Smuggling! Now, I was really scared. "I guess we should go to the police, right?"

Sonia didn't answer for a minute. "I'll tell you what. The diamonds aren't safe in your room. Let's get them, and I'll put them in the hotel safe with my jewelry."

"But I thought you were leaving."

"Well, I can't leave you to handle this by yourself. What kind of a friend would I be if I did that? We have to get to the bottom of this. Let's not tell anybody until I can check out the place where I bought the beads."

"Do you think you ought to go back there?" I asked. "It might be dangerous. Anything could happen."

Sonia's face looked angry. "If somebody is trying to use me to smuggle jewels, I want to find out who it is."

"Me, too. But be careful."

"You're going to sleep in here with me tonight. Jerry can sleep in your room to keep an eye on things. Don't worry. We'll find out what's going on. I'll go see how Jerry's doing and get the diamonds. What about the rest of the beads on that string? Did you open them to see if diamonds were in them, too?"

"No. The bottle's on the table by the bed. The beads are in the plastic bag in the top dresser drawer."

"I'll get the beads and be back in a minute. Don't open the door for anyone but Jerry or me."

"I won't," I said. "And please hurry."

It seemed like hours before Sonia and Jerry came back with my bag.

"Jerry fixed the drain," Sonia said.

"Sonia," I said, "I don't know how to thank you two."

"No thanks are needed." She patted my cheek. "We're just happy we could help."

Jerry smiled and left to go back to sleep in my room.

"I'm sure glad you happened to come by my room. Deanna said you and Jerry left the taverna before the rest of them."

"We did. We came right back to the hotel to pack," she explained. "That's enough talk for now. I want to get up early and put the diamonds in the safe. Then I can start investigating the place where I bought the beads."

I was scared, but I asked, "Could I go with you?"

"It might be better if I go alone. Why don't you meet me in the hotel restaurant around 11:00. I'll tell you what I've found out, and then we can decide what we should do. Okay?"

"Sure," I agreed. "As long as the diamonds are safe."

"And remember not to breathe a word of this to anybody yet."

"Shouldn't we tell Mrs. Foley or Captain Tombazi?" I asked.

She shook her head. "No. Let's hold off until I get a chance to check out the gift shop."

"Can I tell my brother?"

"I don't think so. We don't know what kind of criminals we're dealing with. And Lance is the kind of boy who would try to find out what was going on and get us all in danger."

I had to laugh. "My dad says I'm the one who's always running around like a chicken with its head cut off. Before we left on this trip, he thought I'd get us into trouble."

"It's not your fault. And you did the right thing in telling me about it. Who says you're not a responsible girl? Now, close your eyes, and get some sleep."

She turned off the light. I sat up in bed. "Sonia, shouldn't we open the other beads to see if there are any diamonds in them?"

"I don't think that's a good idea. When we go to the police, it'll be better if we haven't touched them."

I settled back in bed again. I could hear her climbing into the other bed, and I was really glad I wasn't alone. As I lay there feeling safe again, the whole idea of finding the diamonds started to seem more exciting. I couldn't wait to tell Yancey and Deanna and Nicky. I bet even Grandma Lillian had never had anything like this happen to her.

*   *   *   *   *

When I woke up the next morning, Sonia had already left. I found a note propped on the dresser.

Kirstie,
I'll be back by 11:00. I hope I'll have some news. Remember not to say a word to anyone until we know more.

Love,
Sonia

As soon as I was dressed, I hurried back to my room so I could clean up the mess. But

Sonia and Jerry had already cleaned up the water in the bathroom, and there was no sign of makeup on the bed or the floor. My nightgown had been rinsed out and was drying on a hanger.

I was cleaning the blue paint off Sonia's curling iron when Deanna came in. She didn't look at me, she just started changing her clothes.

I sighed. "Deanna, I'm sorry about last night. I promise, I'll never mention Sonia's name or the movie again, okay?"

"Well, I don't know. You'll never keep that promise."

"I'll try. Just give me a chance," I said.

Deanna smiled, and I breathed a sigh of relief. "I guess we can never stay angry with each other for very long," she said.

"How's Mrs. Foley?" I asked.

"She's fine," Deanna answered.

"You should have been here last night." I wanted to make her smile again. I wanted to make her laugh. "I had a nightmare, knocked over Son—some makeup base. It got all over me, so I took a shower." I told her the whole story, all except about the diamonds. "So, there I was locked out of the room and only wearing one of those thin little hotel towels."

Deanna began to laugh, and I felt better.

"You're making this all up," she said.

"I swear, it's true." I crossed my heart. "If I have any more trouble with bathrooms, I may never use one again!"

"How did you get back in? Why didn't you come and get my key?"

"That was where I was headed, but Son—someone came along. I slept in her room last night. She got Je—somebody to get in here and fix the drain."

"Oh, it's okay to say their names. I just got mad last night. I'm sorry," Deanna said.

"Are we still friends?" I asked.

"Friends," she said and gave me a hug. "Hey, we'd better hurry. We're supposed to meet Nicky at 9:30 to go see the windmills."

Uh-oh. I knew she was going to get mad at me again, but what could I do? "I'm sorry, Deanna. I can't go."

"Why not? Do you have something more important to do?"

"It is important, but I can't tell you about it yet."

"It's about that stupid movie again, isn't it? I give up, Kirstie Allen." She grabbed her canvas bag and stormed to the door.

"Deanna, wait. It's not the movie—" The slam of the door cut off my words.

I hoped Sonia and I were doing the right

thing by not going straight to the police. I'd promised Mom and Dad I'd be responsible. But what was the responsible thing to do? I thought and thought about it until I finally told myself to stop worrying. After all, Sonia said I had done the right thing.

Just before 11:00, I went down to the restaurant. Sonia was already there, sitting at a table in the outdoor courtyard. The courtyard was empty, except for some cats. I had to push an orange cat off the chair before I could sit down.

"What did you find out?" I asked in a low voice, although there was no one to overhear us.

"I didn't find out anything good. I checked out the place where I bought the beads, but there was a different person working there. All he would say was that the other man was sick. He wouldn't give me his name or address."

"So, what are we going to do?"

She took a sip of coffee. "Jerry and I know a man who lives here. Maybe he can get the information for us."

"Does he have a black beard and wear mirrored sunglasses?"

Her hand holding the cup stopped in midair. "What?"

"I saw a guy at the airport and then again with Jerry one night. He was on Santorini, too."

She carefully set down the cup, and then gave a little laugh. "Oh, you mean George Spiridakis. He's our agent in the islands. He helps us get permission to film in Greece."

"I figured that's what he was." I laughed. "At first, though, I thought he was following you. He kept showing up everywhere."

"Look, Kirstie, I have to meet Jerry in a few minutes. You order whatever you want. I'll go sign the tab." She picked up her purse. "Now, don't worry. I'm sure George can find out what's going on. If not, we'll go right to the police." She patted my hand. "I'll see you later."

I hadn't eaten breakfast, so I was starved. I was looking over the menu when I heard a cat meow under the table. I leaned over and saw a large straw tote bag, and poking its head out of it was a small kitten.

I reached down and pulled the bag over close to me. "Hey, kitty, kitty, what are you doing in there?" As I lifted the kitten out, I saw a crumpled Greek newspaper, the only other thing in the bag. I wouldn't have thought much about it, but I noticed the date on the paper was July fourth. I remembered that

Jerry had been reading a July fourth newspaper. Was this the same paper? And if it was, why were they saving an old newspaper?

The bag had to be Sonia's. She was still at the desk, so I hurried over to her.

"Sonia? Is this yours?"

"Oh, Kirstie, thank you for finding it. See, didn't I tell you I got into trouble when I hurried too much?"

That made me feel good. Even a perfect person like Sonia could goof up sometimes.

"Jerry gave this bag to me. I'd hate to lose it."

Had Jerry left that paper in the bag when he gave it to Sonia? "You almost had a stowaway," I said to cover my feeling that something was wrong. "A kitten was in it."

She dropped her purse into the tote bag and laughed. "I always leave something behind when I carry more than one thing. I'll see you a little later. And thanks again."

"Sonia?" I wanted to stop her from going to see Jerry and the man with the sunglasses.

"Yes? What is it? I'm in a terrible hurry."

"Just—just be careful."

I watched her hurry out of the restaurant. What was going on, anyhow? A finger of ice raised the hair on my neck. Suddenly, I felt scared, bone-chilling scared.

Ten

FOR a second I just stood there. Something was going on. I knew it. I was really afraid it involved Jerry and George Spiridakis, the creepy man with the beard and sunglasses.

Sonia and I might be in danger.

I wasn't sure what I should do. Sonia had told me to stop and think about the consequences of my actions. I knew I had to tell someone. I rushed upstairs and knocked on Mrs. Foley's door. There was no answer. It seemed like it was easier to say you should do the right thing than it was to actually do it. It was hard to even figure out what was the right thing to do.

Deanna had said that she, Yancey, and Nicky were going to see the windmills. I had to talk to them. Maybe all of us could decide what to do. I grabbed my purse and ran the whole way into town.

The windmills were on a hill behind the main part of town, so I hiked up there. I saw the German family from our tour, but not my brother and friends. Thinking I might run into them by the harbor, I headed back down the hill. I saw a sign for the tourist police and stopped. I thought maybe I should go in and tell them about the diamonds. But if Jerry was involved, I might put Sonia in more danger.

I noticed a sign that had a picture of a telephone on it. Suddenly, I knew who could tell me what to do.

Nervous and scared, I went in and found someone who spoke English. I dug out all my Greek money and put it on the counter. "I want to call La Mira Hospital in California. That's in America," I said. "Is this enough money?"

It was enough for a short call, so I told the man to cut me off whenever I ran out. The call took forever to get through. Finally, someone picked up the phone and said, "It's your nickel. Shoot."

"Grandma Lillian! It's me, Kirstie!" I yelled, afraid she couldn't hear me all the way in California.

"Kirstie, honey, the nurse didn't tell me this was a long distance call. How are you?"

"Grandm—"

111

"I'll bet you're having the time of your life."

"Grandma, I only have—"

"I sent you a letter in care of American Express in Athens. Did you get it?"

"Grandma Lillian! Please listen! I'm—" I looked around to see if anyone could hear me. "I'm in trouble. Big trouble."

"What is it, Kirstie?" Her tone turned serious. "What's wrong?"

I quickly told her about finding the diamonds and about Sonia and Jerry. "Grandma, I don't know what to do. Sonia's gone to talk to the man I think is behind this whole mess, and I'm scared." My voice had gone high and loud. The man at the desk was looking at me, so I tried to smile to show him I was fine.

"Now, calm down, Kirstie. Just let me think. Well, if I were you, I'd..."

"Grandma! Wait! Tell me what to do."

The line was cut off before she could answer. I had run out of money! Almost in tears, I headed for the door. "Is everything all right, Miss?" asked the man who'd helped me with the call.

"Everything's fine," I lied. I was trying my hardest to be responsible, and nothing was going right. I decided to see if anyone at the yacht knew where Nicky and the others might have gone.

112

I ran the whole way. The tour guide was coming down the gangplank. "Irene, I'm looking for Nicky. He's supposed to be with my brother and my friend Deanna."

"You're in luck," Irene said. "They're in the salon."

I rushed into the salon where the three of them were listening to music. I guess I must have looked upset.

"Hey, what's wrong?" Yancey asked.

"Everything." I looked around to see if any of the crew was nearby. "Nicky, is it safe to talk here?"

"Sure. I'm on duty, and nobody else is aboard right now."

I sank down on a chair. I took a deep breath and began telling them about finding the diamonds in the worry beads.

All three of them were grinning. "You found diamonds in some worry beads, huh?" Yancey snickered. "You're getting as bad as Grandma Lillian. Her story about getting kidnapped in the desert by an Arabian sheikh was pretty good, but this one's even wilder."

"I'm telling the truth!" Why couldn't they believe me? "I found two big diamonds."

The smiles disappeared from their faces when they saw that I was starting to cry. "So, where are they now?" Yancey wanted to know.

"You didn't just leave them in the hotel room?"

"No, I hid them in a bottle of makeup," I explained between sobs. "Then I gave them to Sonia to put in the hotel safe."

"You told *her* and not any of us?" Deanna asked.

"Well, yeah. She gave me the beads. She's been trying to check out the place where she bought them, but the guy who sold them to her is gone."

"That's what she says," added Yancey. "What makes you think you can believe her?"

"Because...she...she wouldn't lie to me."

"We have to go to the police," Deanna said.

"I told you I didn't trust that Jerry," Yancey said. "I'll bet he's mixed up in this."

"I just can't figure out why he'd put the diamonds in Sonia's worry beads? After all, they're married." I made a face. "Oh, I wasn't supposed to tell that they're married."

"All the more reason to think she's involved, too," Yancey said.

"Don't be dumb, Lance. Sonia was really angry that someone might use her to smuggle jewels," I said.

Then he frowned. "I don't know why she'd be dumb enough to put the diamonds in *your* beads. I'd be afraid you'd lose them."

Nicky hadn't said anything up to then. But he said, "Kirstie, did it occur to you that Sonia and Jerry might have been using you to smuggle jewels into the U.S.?"

"No! Sonia's my friend. She'd never do anything that dangerous to..." I stopped. I remembered Jerry's words when I stood outside their door. *It's too dangerous to use a kid.* Maybe they hadn't been talking about the movie at all. I pushed that thought out of my head.

"There's something else," I said. I told them about the newspaper Jerry had been reading and how he'd crumpled it up.

"Well, I'm pretty sure the same newspaper was in a new tote bag that Sonia said Jerry had just given to her."

"Any paper can get crumpled," Deanna said.

"I know," I said. "But the date was the same—July fourth. It was easy to remember. Maybe there was something important in the paper on that day."

"I can probably find a copy of it," Nicky said. "I can't leave the yacht, though, until Irene or one of the crew comes back. And I'll have to tell my father about this. He's visiting a friend on the other side of the island."

"I still think we should go to the police,"

Deanna insisted.

Nicky looked troubled. "Let's see what's in that paper first. If we go to the police without some facts, they might keep the Apollo II from leaving Mykonos for several days. Then the passengers would get mad."

"Besides," Yancey put in, "we don't have the diamonds. By now, Sonia and those two guys have probably left the country with the diamonds."

"I was with Sonia only an hour ago."

"Without the diamonds, who'd believe our story?" Yancey muttered. "Boy, are you dumb, or what, Kirstie? You gave the diamonds right back to the people who probably stole them in the first place."

"I'm not dumb! And Sonia didn't set me up."

We kept arguing. I finally put my hands over my ears. "Nobody will ever make me believe that she put the diamonds in the beads and gave them to me."

"I'm going to call my dad," Deanna said. "He'll know what to do." She groaned. "Oh, no, I don't know the name of their hotel. Mrs. Foley has the phone number. Maybe she's back from touring the museums."

I wanted to go find Sonia and warn her about her husband and the bearded man. But

I didn't say anything to the others.

When Irene finally returned, Nicky decided to go find a copy of the newspaper. Deanna said she'd go back to the hotel, call her dad, and see if either Sonia or Jerry had checked out. Yancey went with her.

"We'll all meet back here," Nicky said. "And be careful—especially you, Kirstie. Don't leave the yacht. You know about the diamonds, so you could be in danger."

"They probably figured she'd tell us," Yancey said. "We're all in danger."

They all took off then, leaving me on the yacht staring after them.

I waited until they were out of sight, and then I headed for the main part of town. I wanted to try to find Sonia. I peered into every store and alley, hoping I'd find her. I didn't care what the others thought. Sonia would never put me in danger.

The town was a maze of buildings, one built on top of the other. It took me a long time to check all the places Sonia might be. People bumped me in the crowded alleys, and every time someone bumped me, I expected to feel a gun in my ribs. But there was no sign of Sonia.

Discouraged and tired, I headed back to the yacht. The others weren't back yet, so I sat on deck staring out at the sea. *Why is it so hard to know what to do?*

I don't know how long I had been staring and thinking. I didn't even notice Nicky until he was right next to me. His face was grim as he held up a newspaper. "I hope Deanna gets ahold of her dad. I think we're in big trouble."

"What does it say?" I asked.

"It's just a short article in the international section," Nicky said. "I'll translate it."

He began to read. "'Police in Amsterdam report piracy in the Mediterranean. A yacht carrying a special courier was attacked and sunk. A fortune in diamonds has disappeared. No further information is known at this time, but this is the second similar crime in three months. Police believe an international smuggling ring is involved.'"

Nicky slowly put down the paper. "This is a lot bigger than we thought."

"What's a lot bigger?" we heard from behind us.

We turned to see Deanna and Yancey walking toward us. They looked hot and flustered. They plunked down in chairs. "We couldn't get a taxi, and we had to walk. Mom and Dad weren't at the hotel when I called. They've gone to some other island for the day. I left a message," Deanna explained. "So, what's so big?" Deanna asked again.

Nicky translated the article out loud again.

"My sister doesn't get us mixed up in a little robbery," Yancey added. "Oh, no, she gets us involved with international jewel thieves."

"I don't know why everybody blames me," I said defensively.

We talked some more without really deciding anything. Finally, Nicky said, "It's getting late. We might as well get something to eat. There's a taverna on the waterfront, so we can keep watch for my father."

"Lance, can you loan me some money?" I asked as we walked to the restaurant. "I'm broke."

"What did you do with all of it?"

"I—uh—I called Grandma Lillian today."

"You did what?"

"I thought she might know what to do. But I ran out of money before she could tell me anything."

"Oh, great. She'll tell Mom and Dad, and we'll be grounded for a year."

"You're worrying about getting grounded. *I'm worried about ever getting home again.*"

Yancey and I had lagged behind the others. Nicky and Deanna waited for us to catch up. "We should stay together," Nicky said.

Nobody had much of an appetite, though,

not even Yancey. We sat there in the taverna, not talking, watching the lights of the boats in the harbor.

"It's getting too dark to see if my dad is back," Nicky said. "We'd better get back to the Apollo."

As we were leaving the restaurant, I caught a glimpse of two people coming out of a building a few doors down. The woman was dressed in dark clothes and wearing a Greek fisherman's hat. The man was wearing black pants and a black sweater. "Look," I whispered. "Is that Sonia and Jerry?"

"The guy's not carrying a cane," Yancey said. "And I've never seen Sonia dressed like that."

"Well, I have," I said, remembering her in the hall—was it only last night? So much had happened that it seemed like days ago that I'd found the diamonds.

"Let's follow them," Yancey said and took off after them.

"I don't think we should," Deanna said. "But I'm not staying here by myself," she said and we all began running after Yancey.

Keeping a safe distance behind so they wouldn't see us, we followed them through town to a beach. Sonia and Jerry went into a building. As we got closer, we could see it was a café. Several men were playing cards. We couldn't see Sonia or Jerry.

"What do we do now?" I asked.

"They've probably gone upstairs to the living quarters," Nicky said.

"Let's go around back," Yancey said. "All these places have balconies. Maybe we can climb up the trellis."

"You're as crazy as Kirstie," Deanna said. "There's no way I'm going near that place."

"You can stand watch and whistle if anyone comes out," suggested Yancey.

She didn't like that idea, either, so she came with us. Nicky and I managed to climb up the trellis without falling. Yancey had to help Deanna. She was so scared that she kept losing her grip on the wooden crossbars.

Luckily, the moon hadn't come up yet. Barely breathing, we crouched in the dark at the far edge of the balcony. The balcony door was open, and inside we could see Sonia and Jerry sitting on a sofa.

"I told you it was too dangerous to use that Kirstie brat," Jerry was saying. "Next time, make friends with some old lady, not a kid."

That Kirstie brat! A huge lump settled in my stomach. Tears sprang to my eyes, and I tried to brush them away. Sonia said she was my friend! But it was just a lie. She was using me. I hadn't meant anything to her at all!

"It was an accident that the beads came open," Sonia was saying. Her voice sounded hard and mean, not like it did when she talked to me. "It could have happened with anybody we picked. George did a lousy job of gluing the beads together."

"Well, there's no use arguing about it. We have to figure out how to get rid of the kid."

I felt a scream in my lungs. My breath caught in my throat, and then it closed tight with fear. I couldn't swallow. I looked at Deanna. She was mouthing the words, *no, no.* Nicky took my hand and squeezed it.

"No, Jerry, you're not going to hurt her," Sonia said sharply. "You promised me there wouldn't be any violence."

"That was before the kid found the diamonds. Use your head, Sonia. She can identify us. It's only a matter of time before she talks to the wrong person."

"What do you have in mind?" Sonia asked.

Just then, someone else entered the room, and they all began to speak Greek. We couldn't see the man. We could only hear his deep, hoarse-sounding voice.

Yancey motioned for us to leave. We all stood up carefully. As I turned around, I bumped into a flower pot. We froze.

Eleven

JERRY turned around toward the balcony. "What's that?" he shouted.

I ducked down, even though I knew he couldn't see us on the dark balcony.

"Oh, it's probably a cat," Sonia told him. "They're all over the place."

"I'm going to take a look, anyway," Jerry said.

Yancey grabbed Deanna by the arm. "Let's get out of here," he whispered.

"Somebody's out here! Sonia, get down to the boat and wait for us," Jerry ordered.

We all scrambled down the trellis as fast as we could. Nicky was last, and part way down, the trellis broke loose from the wall. Nicky crashed to the ground.

"I'm okay," he said. "Follow me!"

We had a little head start because Jerry couldn't get down the broken trellis and had to go through the taverna. We raced along the beach, and then Nicky took us through alleys and side streets. I was completely lost.

"I'm exhausted," Deanna gasped. "Can we stop for a minute?"

Nicky slowed down and looked around. "I'm pretty sure we've lost them. But I'm taking us to a safe place to hide for a while. Can you two make it?" he asked Deanna and me.

I nodded wearily. "As long as you know where you're going."

"It's a place I used to play whenever we visited Mykonos. Hardly anybody knows about it."

We rested for a minute, and then we took off up a hill above the town. The moon gave us a little light. Finally, we came to a cave near the top. The opening looked like a black hole. "I'm not going in there," Deanna said. "Let's just go back to the yacht."

"Huh-uh. Jerry will expect us to go either to the hotel or the yacht," Yancey told her. "Nicky's right. We have to stay here until morning."

Nicky nodded. "I'll bet they try to leave the island while it's still dark. Come on. It's not too bad inside."

I wasn't thrilled about going into that black hole. But to make Deanna feel better, I walked right in. I almost yelled as a cobweb brushed across my face. Deanna followed, but she didn't seem too happy about our hiding place. "I wish I were home in my own bed right now," she sniffled. After a while I heard her crying softly, so I put my arm around her.

I shivered in the damp, moldy air. As we sat on the cold stone ground, the fear and excitement drained out of me. Now, I just felt hurt and betrayed.

"I—I'm sorry I got you guys mixed up in all this," I said. "I'll never trust anybody again."

"Kirstie, I know how badly you must feel about Sonia," Deanna said. "I'm sorry."

I looked up quickly, but I couldn't see her face in the dim light. I'd figured she'd never want to speak to me again. "You're not angry?"

"No. I guess I was kind of jealous of all the time you spent with her. I thought she was changing you." She gave a little laugh through her tears. "But you're the same old Kirstie, getting us into trouble again."

"Oh, she was helping me all right. I thought she was perfect." My voice broke. "I was so dumb. I just couldn't believe she'd use me that way."

"But don't forget, she didn't want Jerry to hurt you," Nicky said.

"You know something, Kirstie," Deanna

said. "I still think she liked you."

"Yeah," Yancey put in. "I can't figure out why, but I think she really did."

A wave of warmth welled up inside me, and suddenly the cave was no longer cold. I'd never felt so close to anybody as I did right then to my brother, my old friend, and to Nicky, my new friend. "Thanks, guys. And, Deanna, if we get out of this mess okay, I promise I'll never get you in trouble again."

"Yeah, sure," Deanna said with a laugh. "That's like promising the sun won't rise again."

After that we sat for a long while, not talking much.

"Does anybody know what time it is?" Nicky asked.

Yancey had a watch with a lighted dial. "It's almost midnight," he said. "Do you think they've given up by now?"

"I think we should wait until nearly dawn before we try to go to the yacht," Nicky said. "You three try to get some sleep. I'll guard the entrance."

We all grumbled a little at having to sit in the cold cave for three or four more hours. But at least we were safe there.

The hard stone floor felt as cold as ice. How could we be so hot during the day and so cold at night? After a long time, I guess I must have finally dozed off for a while. A hand shaking my arm woke me up.

"Shhh!" Nicky whispered. "Somebody's coming up the hill."

Two lights swung in mid-air. Then as they grew closer, I could make out two figures.

"Everybody get as far back in the cave as you can!" Nicky whispered. "Don't make a sound. I never thought they'd find this cave!" I could hear the fear in Nicky's voice. I was more afraid than I'd ever been in my life.

We all moved to the back of the cave. I leaned against the damp wall, wishing I could just disappear into the rock. My heart was beating so loudly I thought the two people coming up the hill would hear it for sure. My mind was filled with all the horrible things Jerry and Spiridakis would do to us. I heard Sonia's question to the others in the room above the taverna, What did you have in mind? Were we about to find out?

The lights flashed by the entrance. I took a deep breath. I was sure it was going to be my last one.

"Nicolas!"

"Deanna, are you in there?"

"Daddy!" Deanna jumped up and ran toward the lights. "Is it really you?"

"Papa, we're in here," Nicky called out. He grabbed my hand and pulled me up. "It's okay, Kirstie. We're safe."

I almost collapsed with relief when I saw the captain and Mr. Asbury. I was so happy that I started crying.

"Boy, are we glad to see you," Yancey said. "We thought we were goners."

"How did you ever find us?" Deanna asked.

"It's a long story," Mr. Asbury said, turning to me. "Your grandmother has been calling all day. We'd been out sightseeing and didn't get back until this evening. She told us all about the diamonds. I rented a private plane and a pilot and came right to the hotel."

"Poor Mrs. Foley," Deanna said. "She must have been worried sick."

Mr. Asbury shook his head. "She knew you were with Nicolas, so she didn't get really concerned until about 10:00. By then, Mrs. Asbury and I were on our way here."

"When you didn't come back to the yacht," the captain said, "I called everybody I knew on the island. But no one had seen you. When Mr. Asbury got here, I called the police." He put his arm around Nicky's shoulder. "I know you can take care of yourself, but not when you're up against smugglers. I'm glad I remembered this cave."

"Papa," Nicky said, "we have to find Miss Loring and Mr. Burke before they get off the island."

"The police are already looking for them," the captain said.

"I gave the police a good description of them, but we need to know what the third man looks like."

"I can tell you that," I said. "I think he's Greek. He's hulky-looking and holds his arms out kind of like an ape. He has a black beard and wears mirrored sunglasses, even at night."

"You took some pictures of him at that café on Santorini," Deanna said.

"I got plenty of pictures of Sonia, too," Yancey said. "You can take the tapes."

"I think we should get right back to the Apollo," the captain said. "The police may have heard something by now."

With everybody talking at once about what had happened to us, we headed back to the yacht. Deanna's mother was waiting at the top of the gangplank. She hugged Deanna, and then she looked at us. "Are you children all right?"

"Yes," I said. "But we were really scared."

We all went into the salon where Irene made hot chocolate to warm us up. I huddled in the corner, thinking about Sonia. Deanna sat next to me. "Don't feel bad, Kirstie. Sonia's not worth it."

"I know. It's not just her. I've spoiled the trip for everybody. If I hadn't been so impressed by a movie star, I never would have been fooled by her."

Deanna didn't say anything. But I just knew things were all right between us. After all, we were best friends.

* * * * *

The sky was just turning pinkish gray when the police arrived. They spoke to the captain in Greek, and then he translated for us. "There's good news," he said. "They caught Burke and George Spiridakis. They had the diamonds on them. But the bad news is that a fisherman saw a jet boat take off with an American woman at the wheel. Her description will be sent to all the islands."

"But Nicky said there are three thousand islands. She could be anywhere! They'll never find her," I said.

After the police left, I apologized to everybody. "This whole thing is my fault. I'm sorry."

"That's nonsense," Mrs. Asbury said. "It could have happened to anyone."

"No, it's my fault. I was so stupid to think she really liked me. And the worse thing is that it may not be over yet. I gave Sonia my address and phone number."

"Yes, but you have hers, too," Deanna reminded me.

"It's probably not her real address," Mr. Asbury said.

Mrs. Foley put her arm around me. "This must have been awful for you—alone with those diamonds. I wish you'd told me about them."

"Or the police," Mr. Asbury said.

"That was my fault," said Nicky. I saw that he didn't look at his father when he explained. "I was afraid the tour would be held up and we'd lose all our passengers. I'm sorry, Papa."

"You kids try to rest for a few hours," Mr. Asbury said. "We're flying back to Athens today."

I glanced at Nicky and saw that he was looking at me. Would I ever see him again?

He came over to me and whispered, "Let's go talk."

I nodded and followed him out onto the deck. Neither of us said anything for a while. We just watched the harbor become light as the sun rose.

He spoke first, but I could tell he was kind

of embarrassed. "Kirstie, I just wanted you to know this was the best tour ever." He didn't look at me as he said softly, "I'm going to miss you."

"Me, too," I said. "I thought I might be coming back to do that stupid movie, but now..."

"Maybe you and your grandmother can come back. You said she loved Greece."

"Maybe we can. And I can ask Mr. Asbury about your coming to California. Lance is right. You could be a great swimmer with the right coaching."

"Kirstie, until we do see each other again, I—uh—I want to give you something to remember me by."

Nicky took off the chain with the little silver dolphin and handed it to me. "Will you wear it?"

"I sure will, Nicky," I said, feeling tears in my eyes.

He took the chain from my hand and fastened it around my neck.

"I love it, Nicky," I said. "Thank you."

"Don't forget me," Nicky said. "Someday, I'm sure we'll meet again."

The gentle lapping of the waves against the boat seemed to echo Nicky's voice saying, *Someday, we'll meet again.*

Twelve

ON the plane back to Athens, I looked out the window, thinking about Nicky and holding the little silver dolphin.

"Where did you get that?" Deanna asked.

"Hey, that's Nicky's," Yancey piped up. "I remember him wearing it when we went swimming."

I didn't say anything. It was like I was thinking about Nicky and Greece and everything, and I didn't want to talk just then.

Yancey said, "It would be great if Nicky could come to California sometime."

That reminded me of what I'd told Nicky. I tapped on Mr. Asbury's shoulder. "Could I talk to you about something for a minute?"

I told him about Nicky and how good a swimmer he was. "He's won a lot of medals, but he's never had any real coaching. And you've had exchange students live with you before. I was just wondering if you could work something out with him? With good coaching, he could make the Olympic team."

"I'll think about it, Kirstie," he said. "But I have some bad news to tell you kids. I might as well get it over with now."

My stomach did a nosedive. What had happened now?

"I'm afraid the yacht isn't going to be repaired in time for us to use it this vacation. We thought we'd look around Athens and then head home in a few days."

"I know you're all disappointed," Mrs. Asbury said. "Maybe we can come back next year."

I didn't feel as bad about it as I thought I would. So much had happened that it seemed as if we'd been gone for two months. "I don't mind, as long as you invite me next year."

"It's a date," Mr. Asbury said, looking relieved that we weren't upset.

As soon as we got to the hotel in Athens, Mr. Asbury went to the police to see if there was any word about Sonia. He took the video tapes to help identify her. When he returned, he said there was no news about her. Maybe it was wrong to think it, but deep down I almost hoped they would never catch Sonia.

The next morning I asked Mr. Asbury if we could go to the American Express office to pick up my letter from Grandma Lillian. When we got there, I saw that the place was full of older kids carrying backpacks and standing in line to pick up their mail from home. Watching the older kids, I got a lump in my throat. Suddenly, I missed my mom and dad and grandma. With everything that had happened on this trip, I hadn't had time to feel homesick.

Deanna and Yancey stopped to talk to some kids who had "San Diego, USA" written on their backpacks. As I headed over to the mail window to get my letter, I noticed an old woman in line at another window. She was dressed in black, with a peasant scarf over her gray hair, and funny white stockings. She was carrying a string of amber beads.

She glanced at me, and her dark eyes caught mine for a brief second. Then she turned away.

She dropped the beads into her bag and shoved her hands into her pockets—but not before I saw her long fingernails. Long fingernails! Something was wrong with those fingernails. No old Greek peasant woman would have fingernails like that!

Could it be Sonia?

The woman had dark eyes, not brilliant green. But people can wear colored contact lenses, can't they? Sonia would never show herself in public without a disguise. Something inside me knew it was her.

I didn't know what to do. What was the responsible thing, the right thing? It would be so easy to let her just walk away. Nobody but me would ever know. Deanna said Sonia liked me. And Sonia did tell Jerry not to hurt me.

But Sonia had chosen me to smuggle the diamonds. *She* was the one who got me mixed up in all this. *She* was the one who put me in danger.

The woman started to hobble away. She looked so old. Maybe I was wrong. No. Sonia was an actress.

Almost in tears, I crossed over to her and tapped her shoulder. "Wait," I said.

She turned to face me. Her eyes were questioning. "No speak English," she said in a shaky voice with a strong accent.

"You can cut the act, Sonia. I know it's you."

She took a deep breath, and sighed. "How? How did you know?"

"You should have cut your fingernails," I said.

"Kirstie, I'm sorry you got involved in this."

I wanted so much to believe Sonia, but I told myself not to listen to her. "Why did you do this to me?" I asked. "I thought we were friends."

"We are friends." Sonia reached out to take my hand, but I jerked it back. "Didn't I tell you that you reminded me of my little sister?"

"Which one?" I asked sarcastically. "Jeanie or Janie? I bet you lied about that. You've probably never even had a sister."

"You must hate me, but I want you to know I would never have let anybody hurt you."

"Hey, Kirstie, did you get your letter yet?" Yancey called.

Sonia and I both swung around to see Yancey and Deanna coming toward us.

Sonia gripped my wrist. "What are you going to do?" she asked.

Her fingernails were digging into my skin. "You're hurting me, Sonia."

As Deanna and Yancey came up to us, Sonia let go of my hand. In broken English, she said, "I tell fortune. Only 50 drachma. Yes?"

I forced a smile at Yancey. "I'd love to have my fortune told." Then I said something to him in our secret language that nobody but he and I could understand.

"That sounds like fun," he said, playing along, but I knew he hadn't recognized Sonia.

"I'll go get some money from Mr. Asbury."

Deanna realized something was going on, but she didn't say anything.

For the first time, Sonia looked worried. "Must go now," she said. "I meet you later."

"You never did answer my question. Why did you set me up like that, Sonia?"

"Sonia!" Deanna cried. "You're craz—" She peered into Sonia's face. "Is that really you?"

"Yeah, it's her," I said. Then I looked at Sonia again. "Why, Sonia? Why did you pretend to be my friend?"

"It was Jerry," she said quickly. "He chose you. He needed to raise money to produce his movie. He forced me to go along with the smuggling scheme."

Deanna snorted with disgust.

"Kirstie, I admit that at first we were just using you. But when I got to know you, I begged Jerry to find someone else. By now, you should know that I'd never have let anyone harm you."

I nodded slowly. "I do know that. But there are other kinds of hurts. I know—"

"No! Don't listen to her, Kirstie," Deanna broke in. "Don't you ever learn? She's a crook and a liar."

"Kirstie!" Sonia's voice was pleading. "I don't have the diamonds. My career is already ruined." Tears came to her eyes. "Just let me walk out of here, please."

Part of me wanted to say, *run, Sonia!* But part of me wondered if her tears were only the tears of an actress.

"Boy, it's too bad your movie career is over," Deanna said. "You could get an Oscar for this performance. I'm going to get the police."

I turned to look for Yancey. He was coming through the door with two men in uniform. "You don't need to get the police, Deanna," I said. Then I turned to Sonia and said, "I'm sorry, Sonia. I already sent Lance to get help. I told him in our secret language."

Her shoulders sagged. Before the police took her away she said, "No matter what you think, Kirstie, I didn't lie about one thing. You were very special to me."

It was really weird. Knowing Sonia had helped me become more responsible. She had taught me a lot about feeling better about myself. The old Kirstie would have helped Sonia get away. But now I knew that I had done the right thing, the responsible thing.

I wished things could have worked out differently. As I watched the police take Sonia away, I couldn't swallow the huge lump in my throat. I couldn't blink back the tears in my eyes.

* * * * *

After about nine hours in the air, we finally landed at the Los Angeles airport, where the Asburys' private jet was waiting for us. Even the short trip to Rancho La Mira took too long. I was so anxious to see my family.

As the plane circled the airport, Yancey cried, "Look at the crowd out there! I wonder what's going on."

"Maybe somebody tried to cross the runway," Deanna said, jabbing me in the ribs.

The plane landed. "I can see Mom and Dad. And there's Grandma Lillian!" I yelled, looking out the little window. "She's out of the hospital."

As we came down the steps, the crowd pushed through the gate and surrounded us. Some kids from our school were carrying a huge banner. It read "WELCOME HOME HEROES."

Yancey grinned. "I think they mean us!"

Then Yancey and I were being hugged by Mom and Dad and Grandma.

"Grandma Lillian, you're out of the hospital," I said.

"No, I'm orbiting the moon," she said, teasing me. "Of course, I'm out of the hospital. No phoofdiddley hip is going to keep me from enjoying my grandchildren's celebration."

"If you hadn't called Mr. Asbury, we might not even be here now," I said.

"Honey," Mom said. "We're so proud of you. The way you helped catch those smugglers was great."

I glanced at Deanna and Yancey, but I couldn't look at my parents' faces. "I—uh—if it hadn't been for me, we wouldn't have been involved in the whole mess. I know I deserve to be punished."

Before they could answer, the crowd that had stood back while we greeted our family pressed forward. Everybody was shouting questions at once.

"Kirstie, will you have to go back to Greece for the trial?" a reporter asked.

Mr. Asbury answered that for me. "No, none of us will. The smugglers were caught with the diamonds on them. They were first-time criminals, and they may get off with an easy sentence because they gave information to help break a large smuggling ring."

"Kirstie, were you scared that they might kill you?" somebody called out.

"Kirstie, how does it feel to be a real-life heroine?"

I reached out for Deanna's and Yancey's hands and held them up beside me. "All three of us, plus a Greek boy named Nicolas Tombazi, helped catch the smugglers. But what I want to know is, how did you know about this?"

Grandma Lillian beamed. "When Deanna's dad called to tell us that you had nabbed that woman crook," she explained, "I phoned the newspaper and gave them an interview." She held out a copy of the *La Mira Journal.*

"Grandma, I didn't 'nab' anybody. I told you Deanna and Lance did as much or more than I did."

I looked down at the newspaper. The huge headline read, LOCAL KIDS CATCH SMUGGLERS IN GREECE.

Deanna, Yancey, and I looked at the newspaper. Below the headline was a picture of the three of us that my mom had taken last fall in our backyard.

"It's too bad Nick isn't here," said Yancey. "He really deserves a lot of the credit."

I touched the little silver dolphin that was hanging around my neck. "You know what?" I said softly as the crowd started cheering some more. "I have a feeling he will be here sometime."

About the Author

ALIDA YOUNG and her husband live in the high desert of southern California. When she's not writing or researching a new novel, or taking long hikes in the desert, she likes to travel. She took a trip around the world with her son. "My very favorite place was Greece," she says. "A lot of the things that happen to Kirstie in this book actually happened to me. I had a lot of trouble with Greek toilet handles, just like Kirstie," Alida explains. "And I had some trouble with the locks on the doors, too."

But there's one thing in *Summer Cruise, Summer Love* that didn't happen to Alida. "I did take a donkey ride," she says. "But the awful thing that happened to Kirstie didn't happen to me! Thank goodness!"